Mary Ann Walker

Leaves from the Backwoods

Mary Ann Walker

Leaves from the Backwoods

ISBN/EAN: 9783744642361

Printed in Europe, USA, Canada, Australia, Japan

Cover: Foto ©Andreas Hilbeck / pixelio.de

More available books at **www.hansebooks.com**

Leaves

from the

Backwoods.

—I hope as no unwelcome guest
At your warm fireside, when the lamps are lighted,
To have my place reserved among the rest,
Nor stand as one unsought and uninvited.

LONGFELLOW.

Montreal:
PRINTED BY JOHN LOVELL, ST. NICHOLAS STREET.
1861.

CONTENTS.

PART I.

The Year.

And this our life, exempt from public haunt,
 Finds tongues in trees, books in the running brooks;
Sermons in stones, and good in everything.

AS YOU LIKE IT.

Leaves from the Backwoods.

CHRISTMAS MIDNIGHT CHIMES.

Ring out, ring out, ye joyous bells, and make the hills resound,
Cast forth upon the waters dark, your glad exulting sound;
Tell the good tidings far and wide, let all the people know
Christmas is come, the time of joy, of rest from care and woe.

Send loud your notes, where, round the hearth, the scattered
children meet,
And wait, as in the olden days, your earliest chime to greet;
Re-echo through the brightened room, blend with each loving
tone,
Wake in each heart a joy as great, as pure as childhood's own

With softened distance-mellowed tone, fall on the listening ear
Of him, whom rolling seas divide from all he holds most dear;
Let the loved voices of his home, come mingled with your peal,
Kind wishes for the Christmas time, prayers offered for his
weal.

Float round the sufferer's bed with yet a softer, holier swell;
Repeat the tale of Love Divine, a Saviour's advent tell;
Bid him remember, Who was born, that he might be forgiven,
Bid him look up from earthly pain, to peace and rest in heaven.

Oh bells, for me ye have a tone, an echo of the past,
Yet breathe it not to other hearts, a shade o'er them to cast
How softly, musically sad! how silver sweet and low!
A sigh from the departing year, that sorroweth to go.

THE VIGIL OF THE SHEPHERDS.

O'er Judah's quiet hills, from height to height
Drooped slowly down, the curtains of the night,
In matchless beauty, gemmed with stars of light.

Seated beneath the shadow of the rocks,
Their shelter from the heat or tempest's shocks,
A band of shepherds watched their slumbering flocks.

Deep stillness hung above them, such as reigns
In those calm hours, when night in silence wanes,
And men in deepest sleep lose joys and pains.

Till, turning to the glory of that sky,
Of Israel's royal bard the numbers high,
Broke from their lips at once in melody.

Then, loud and clear, they sang with glad acclaim,
"The heavens, O Lord! on high declare Thy fame,
The firmament extols Thy glorious name!

Day speaketh of Thee to the coming day,
And night, whose countless orbs Thy word obey,
Doth to the following night Thy praise display."

Thus ceased the song, and echo scarce was still,
When broke a sudden light upon the hill,
And fear shook every heart with trembling thrill.

Silent as thought—unheralded—alone,
An angel stood, a glory round him shone ;
He spoke, and heavenly love inspired his tone.

"Fear not," he said, "let Earth rejoice and sing ;
To you, and all mankind glad news I bring ;
To-day, at length, is born your promised King.

Go, and in Bethlehem, in a manger laid,
Find Him, by whom both heaven and earth were made,
Emanuel, Prince of Peace, in flesh arrayed."

Then, with a flood of light, and burst of sound,
A thousand angel forms were seen around,
Angels, with beauty clad, with glory crowned.

"Glory to God on high!" aloud they sung,
Till heaven's blue arches with the anthem rung,
And, "Peace on earth!" re-echoed every tongue.

Lovelier than sunset hues on lake and hill,
Music and light grew fainter, lovelier, till
The stars shone out again, and all was still.

Then each to each the shepherds, turning slow
From that bright vision, spake in accents low,
"What thing is this? To Bethlehem let us go."

THE STAR OF THE MAGI.

In those blue skies afar,
I see a single solitary star,
Its radiant light
So far from earth, so calmly, purely bright.

And even so, I dream,
Fell on the wise men's eyes that mystic beam,
Which, from their home,
Led them, through Judah's destined land to roam.

Oft, as they journeyed on,
Their glance was raised to where serenely shone
That silent star,
Leading their steps so surely, though so far.

What thoughts, unknown before,
Stirred in those minds, so rich in earth's deep lore!
What did they seek?
A King's new-risen pomp? an infant Saviour meek!

And when the city spread
Its silent streets before them, in the dead,
Calm hush of night,
Above what palace roof shone that celestial light?

Soon had the star its rest;
Still beamed its glittering orb on heaven's pure breast,
But all its rays
Fell on a lowly spot, dim in that shadowy place.

They passed the humble door
They bent undoubting, gladly to adore,
The Virgin's Son;
They knew the King they sought, they knew their journey done.

Thou Star of Heavenly birth,
So guide us, wandering through the dark of earth,
Until we rest
Before Thy changeless throne, O God for ever blest!

THE SLEIGH RIDE.

O'er the smooth and glittering snow,
Merrily, merrily off we go—
Nature sleeps, and not a sound
Breaks the stillness all around,
While the horses' feet keep time
To the sleigh bells' tuneful chime.

Now we pass the village street,
Where the varying pathways meet;
Now across the fields we fly,
Where the wild flowers buried lie;
Buried, in their shroud of snow,
Till the summer breezes blow.

Now we gain the frozen stream,
Where the icy atoms gleam;
Say, could they have brighter been
Were they gems to deck a queen?
Who would deem that down below
Still the rapid waters flow?

Here, the rocks rise tall and black,
Casting shadows o'er our track ;
There, the golden sunbeams rest
On the mountain's sparkling breast ;
While above us, meets the eye,
Clear and deep, the azure sky.

Now we take the homeward way,
Warned by the departing day ;
From the windows, o'er the snow,
See the bright fires' ruddy glow ;
Their mute welcome seems akin
To the faces bright within.

A HAPPY NEW YEAR.

A glad good morrow ! neighbour mine,
A good new year to thee !
A year of life, and health and hope,
I pray that it may be.

Last year we held each other's hand,
The self-same wish had we,
And has it not been well fulfilled ?
Thank God ! it has to me.

We did not wish that we might have
  A summer all the year,
That winter's storms and autumn's blasts
  Might never hover near.

And though they came—the rainy days,
  Fierce storms, and bitter wind—
They passed, and left our sky, perhaps,
  More brightly blue behind.

So we will hope the opening year,
  Whose morning is so bright,
May have a smiling dawn to give,
  For every stormy night.

And should Life's evening shadows close,
  And Death's dark night draw near,
It shall but be the harbinger
  Of Heaven's unclouded year.

MAY BLOSSOMS.

What gift shall we bring thee, sweet Queen of the May,
What flower from the fields shall we offer to-day?
Shall we seek for the violet, new sprinkled with dew?
Thy blue eyes will rival its loveliest hue.

Shall we steal from its spray the first rose that has given
Its delicate breath to the breezes of heaven?
Those sun-tinted petals thy breast may enshrine,
Its bloom and its beauty are emblems of thine.

From grass-covered banks, where each breeze softly sighs,
We'll bring thee the harebell, that mirrors the skies,
So fragile and fair—yet the tempest sweeps o'er,
And though it may bend, it will smile as before.

And under green shadows, deep hid from the sun,
Where, hushed into silence, the streams softly run,
We'll seek the pure lilies, whose blossoms will shine
More lovely than pearls on those tresses of thine.

But, meadow and grove! though ye yield from your store
Grace, beauty, and fragrance, ye cannot do more;
They are fading, and autumn will bear them away,
But hers are the charms that can never decay.

SPRING.

I thought thou couldst not fail to wake,
Sweet Spring, an answering chord in me;
I thought 'twas but my harp to take,
And I could win a song from thee.

Alas! unworthy of thy smile,
Unworthy, must the minstrel be,
Whom even thou canst not beguile,
To whom thou bring'st no melody.

Yet I have loved thee—Can it be,
Time's ruthless hand has robbed my heart
Of all the warmth that welcomed thee?
Of all the joy thou couldst impart?

No! but my thoughts so long have dwelt
On daily life's most sordid things,
That half thine influence is unfelt,
My harp is robbed of half its strings.

But bring, O music-breathing air!
One strain I loved in days gone by,
My sleeping muse shall wake more fair,
Responsive to its hallowed sigh.

EVENING HYMN AT SEA.

Oh, be Thou near us—on the ocean's breast
The ship lies tranquil, as a child at rest:
If Thou a watch above our slumbers keep,
On the calm sea we may as calmly sleep.

Oh, be Thou near us! if the storm should rise,
And dreadful lightnings fire the angry skies,
'Mid tempest's rage, if Thou art near us still,
Our steadfast hearts shall fear no threatening ill.

Oh, be Thou near us! if this silent wave
For one of us should be th' appointed grave,
To Thee alone, the parting soul may cry,
And if Thou answer, who would fear to die?

Oh, be Thou near us! then whatever fate,
Fixed by Thy gracious hand, may us await,
Secure in Thee, our souls shall find repose,
And calm, untroubled sleep our eyelids close.

THE ROSES.

Take these Roses; they are fair,
And glittering yet with morning dew;
They'll bloom unchanged through noonday's glare,
Nor lose their scent or hue.
They may lose the sparkling dew,
May want the freshness of the morn,
Yet, all the sunny hours through,
Thy breast they will adorn.

But, ere evening shadows close,
Cast those worthless flowers away;
While the bloom is on the rose,
Ere sinks the god of day.
Here's another simpler flower—
When night shall reign with silent sway,
This blossom, cherished till that hour,
Shall well thy care repay.

Like these flowers, the hearts that throng
Round thee in thy fair young day,
Some will share thy sunshine long,
At nightfall drop away.

Some there are, whose modest worth,
Scarcely known in daylight's glare,
Shall brighten all the darkening earth
In hours of pain and care.

SEEKING.

Why is this stupendous intelligence so retired and silent, while present in all the scenes of the earth, and in all the paths and abodes of men?

FOSTER.

Where dost Thou dwell,
Unknown, unseen, yet knowing, seeing all?
We find Thee not in hermit's lonely cell,
Nor lofty palace hall.

No more at eve
Thy form is with us on the dusty road,
The dead sleep on, though loving hearts may grieve;
The suffering bear their load.

Night closes round—
In the green forest aisles no leaf is stirred;
So hushed, as if heaven's distant music sound
Might even here be heard.

Through all we see,
Up to the azure roof with stars inwrought,
Through all Earth's temple, do we look for Thee;
Alas! we find Thee not.

Yet, Thou art near;
Father! forgive our weak and failing sight;
Forgive, and make our darkness noonday clear
With Thy celestial light.

Thy love has given
Faith's telescope, wherewith to gaze on Thee;
Aid us, that through it looking unto Heaven,
Thy glory we may see.

SUMMER HYMN.

Hark! Earth begins her matin hymn;
The wide expanse of hill and plain,
The river, and the mountain breeze
Uniting, swell the glad refrain;
Day, throned upon the eastern heights,
From herb and flower, bids incense rise
To mingle in the azure heaven,
With Nature's wordless harmonies.

All things—the insect world around,
The squirrels peeping from the shade,
The birds that warble on the boughs,
The herds amid the sunshine laid ;
All living things, and all beside,
Thy works, whate'er their form may be,
Varied by Thy creating hand,
Are one, O God, in praising Thee.

Nor, Father ! let thy latest born,
The chosen object of thy care,
Contemn the universal hymn
That nature raises everywhere.
For blessings of the opening year,
For spring and summer's sunny days,
And for the harvest's promised store
Accept, O Lord, our grateful praise.

THE RIVER.

I stand upon the river's side,
And at my feet the rapid tide
  Goes wandering onward ceaselessly;
So clear, so bright its waters gleam,
That, mirrored in the crystal stream,
  I see each neighbouring object lie.

Yon cottage with its mantling vine
And roses that around it twine,
  Has its bright copy in the wave;
Those trees, that by the margin grow,
Cast each its shadow down below,
  As, bending o'er, their boughs they lave.

And yet the current hurries on;
Not here, it knows its journey done,
  Though fair and sweet the scene may be,
Though darkling forests lie before,
And channelled rocks, and chasms hoar;
  Its rest is only in the sea.

But many another grassy mead
Shall greet it, in its onward speed,
And there the grateful stream shall pay,
With added freshness, every leaf,
Even, as here, its sojourn brief
Sheds brighter, fresher bloom to-day,

So mortals, by life's current strong,
Perchance unwilling, borne along,
May hear the river's wordless speech,
"Sunshine and summer days are thine,
They cheer thy way, but why repine
When storms their sterner lessons teach?

And when, awhile, thy path may lead
Through soft and tranquil paths, take heed
The grateful stream is type of thee;
The gifts to thee so freely given,
As freely render back to Heaven,
In works of love and charity."

TO AN ORIOLE.

SEEN MAY, 1861.

Why from thy southern home,
  Why dost thou roam so far?
Thou art too bright to come
  Thus, like a wandering star,
    To these cold shores of ours.

Oh, quickly spread thy wing,
  Linger no longer here,
Haste, ere the night shall bring
  Chill that thou couldst not bear,
    Back to thy land of flowers!

Haste! though the charmèd eye,
  Rests on thy glowing plume,
Haste! let me see thee fly;
Seek'st thou a living tomb?
    This is no place for thee!

Lured by that splendour rare,
  Soon may some thoughtless heart
Doom thee, bright bird, to bear
  The prisoner's hopeless part—
            Fly, whilst thou yet are free!

Back on thine airy way,
  Vision of beauty! go,
Till thy tired pinions stay,
  Where thine own summers glow!
            There thou mayst fearless rest.

Bright visitant, farewell!
  Far in thy native bowers,
Thou mayst thy comrades tell,
  Sad are the exile's hours;
            Home, home alone is blest!

THE EVENING WALK.

Here, let us rest awhile ;—this moss grown trunk
Makes a luxurious seat, a throne, if e'er
Thrones are so free from care, as we may be
In this our rustic palace ; high o'erhead
The arching boughs, that hold our roof of leaves,
Mock man's laborious tracery, and show
A mightier Architect—no windows throw,
Though stained with loveliest hues, a light so pure,
So cool, so chaste, as, through the fluttering screen,
Steals down upon the flowers, and lends them grace,
Down in yon hollow, hidden by the fern,
The noisy brook goes rushing on its way ;—
The bee, unwearied by his day of toil,
Comes home rejoicing, with his fragrant load,
The woodpecker sends echoes through the wood ;
And timid squirrels, with their shining eyes,
Peep at us from among the withered leaves.
The bolder chitmonk sits upon a bough
And eyes us steadily—his small, shrill bark
Startling the birds upon their lofty perch.

Look at these flowers;—our English flowers are fair,
And their familiar faces stir our hearts,
But these are different;—See, this one has leaves
Like the white water-lily, fragile, pure
And shattered by a touch;—a crimson stain
Is on each petal, as some wounded heart
Had shed its lifeblood o'er the snowy cup,
And dyed it thus for ever. Here is one
Alike in shape, but of a purple hue;
And this might be a lily of the vale
Grown to gigantic size—the shining leaves
Have lost in width, what they have gained in height,
But the flowers keep their semblance. I have seen
This plant before—last year we found the roots,
But it was later, and the bloom was gone;
Where the bells had been, scarlet berries hung,
Warm, glowing, in the shadows of the wood.

Here, are some yellow violets—not like those
We used to love; these have no sweet perfume,
And their pale hue looks strange, unnatural;
And here, are white and blue, but all alike
Strange to our eyes, and speechless to our hearts.

I like this lilac-tinted flower that creeps
Close to the ground—Titania might have wreathed
Its tiny blossoms in her hair; and sweet,
Though faint, the odour that betrays its nook,
The only scented wild-flower we have found.
Here, are more fairy blossoms, white as snow,
Gleaming like stars, that, tempted by the flowers,
Wandering from yon blue heaven above us spread,
Were caught among the leaves.—How exquisite
The form and veining of each silvery gem!

How softly fades the twilight! But the night,
Though lovely, must not find us lingering here.
The moon will gild the treetops, and the stars
Shine on the dewy flowers, and on our seat,
While we turn homeward with our gathered wealth;
Our gleaming wealth of jewels richly wrought,
Gems eloquent to speak the Graver's praise.

THE SONG OF THE SEA.

List to their music,
Mournfully swelling—
What is the tale,
That those waters are telling?
Thou, who hast heard them,
By night and by day,
Answer—those waves,
Canst thou tell what they say?

Yes! I will teach thee
The song that they sing
To the ship on the sea,
To the bird on the wing;
Oft have I heard it
Mid darkness and storm,
Or caught its low voice
On the breath of the morn.

Short is their lesson
And easy to say,
This all they utter,
" Passing away !"
Each wave, as it rises
And dies on the shore,
Still repeats only
These words evermore.

Heed thou the warning;
Young though thou be,
The sun of to-morrow
May ne'er rise for thee ;
And, though thou shouldst linger
For many a day,
Yet hopes, joys, affections,
Are passing away.

FLOWERS.

Oh, bring me, bring me flowers, from my own dear land again,
I feel as if their well-known scents would charm away my pain,
Their forms would bring me back the dreams of childhood's
happy days,
Like visions of the night, lit up by fancy's sparkling rays.

Oh, let me feel the perfume of the violet in the air,
And clasp within my weary hand the primrose pale and fair,
The mayflower's gorgeous leaves of gold, that decked our
youthful queen,
The sorrel's snowy petals, hid among its leaves of green.

Bring me the dark blue hyacinth, that studded all the grass,
Where we, beneath the elm trees' shade, the joyous hours
would pass;
The roses, that around our bower, their thousand blossoms shed,
Or mingled with the stately boughs, that arched it overhead.

Oh, let me wreathe once more the flowers, I ever loved the best,
The gay and fragrant hawthorn, in its springtide beauty drest;
The brilliant pansies—flowers of thought—like thoughts that
quickly die,
The fragile harebell, ringing forth its fairy melody.

My eyes grow dim with unshed tears, the tears of vain regret,
Oh, flowers of home, in many a dream, your bright forms
haunt me yet,
But never, never more amid your beauties may I stand,
Or lay ye on my heart again, gems of my fatherland!

THE LAND OF REST.

Where art thou, land of rest?
Oft, amid evening skies,
Rich outlines, as of dwellings blest,
Before my vision rise,
But ah! they fade as night draws on,
They fade, they pale, as sinks the sun.

When morning beams are bright,
The distant mountain slopes,
All bathed in soft and tender light,
Seem fair as youth's fond hopes;
But noon must steal their brave array,
And leave them cold, and stern, and grey.

Oh, distant, yet beloved,
Art thou, that seem'st so fair ;
Nought but a poet's fancy vain,
A phantom of the air ?
Never to bless the longing sight,
With all thy fulness of delight ?

What though, in passing dream,
The weary tread thy shore,
Bathe in thy rivers' tranquil stream,
And learn thy sacred lore,
Day calls them back, to meet again
Their daily toil, their daily pain.

VISIONS.

I have dreamt of a home in a changeless clime,
Where nought that we loved was the spoil of Time;
Where the summer breezes' gentle wings
Brought to our dwelling all lovely things;
And life was bliss on that happy shore—
I've dreamt;—but I see the bright vision no more.

I dream no more of a golden age,—
I have learned a lesson from life's dark page;
Flowers may bud, and bloom, and die;
Storms may darken the summer sky;
But not in skies, or in withering flowers,
Is the saddest change;—for that change is ours

Day by day, as our life glides past,
Something must leave us that graced the last;
Some rose of hope, from its stem is shed;
Some bud of fancy, falls pale and dead;
Till nought is left, but the scentless bloom
That memory plants by affection's tomb.

THE BRIDAL.

Weave the garlands bright and gay,
For the bride, to-morrow;
Raise the festal arches high,
For the bride, to-morrow;
Deck the church with laurel boughs,
Seek the myrtle, where it grows,
Lilies, for the sunny brows
Round the bride, to-morrow.

See! they fade, the flowers ye bring,
For the bride, to-morrow;
Little fragrance they shall fling,
Round the bride, to-morrow;
Cast them forth, and bring, instead,
Yew, that mourneth for the dead,
Twine dark ivy overhead,
For the bride, to-morrow.

Useless all your care shall be,
For the bride, to-morrow;
He, the bridegroom that hath wooed,
Stays not for to-morrow;

'Neath his kiss, her lips grow pale,
And her fluttering pulses fail,
Loud and deep shall be the wail,
Round her grave, to-morrow..

MORNING.

Morning! whose earliest, purest ray,
Sheds beauty on the distant hills,
And whose light winds the treetops sway
Above the newly wakened rills,
Many a bright floweret opens to thy smile,
And thy sweet spells, from sleep, all living things beguile.

Delightful hour! the first, the best,
The brightest, in glad summer's train,
When man, refreshed by peaceful rest,
Blithely resumes his toil again;
Hope's angel—smiles through all thy beauties shine,
And all her charms, sweet morning hour, are thine.

NIGHT.

Oh, loveliest hour of all that bless
Earth with their passing loveliness,
Calm night ! when, sinks in deep repose,
Each care, each toil, that daylight knows ;
To me, than summer's noonday glare,
More dear thou art, more sweetly fair.

Canst thou be all of earth, when, oft
Upon the heart, thine influence soft
Falls, as, from heaven, a healing shower,
So strangely deep its soothing power ?
And must thy beauty pass away,
Thy softness yield to lasting day ?

Yes ! night, thy reign must soon be o'er ;
Thy calm shall soothe the heart no more ;
Thy task fulfilled, thy mission done,
When Earth, its latest course, has run,
No need for night ; no need for rest,
When Heaven's own glory fills the breast.

EVENING TIME.

" At evening time there shall be light."
Yes, when old age shall come
And night's dark shades obscure the path,
Whereon we're travelling home ;
When, 'wildered by the gathering gloom,
Appalling fears arise,
The first pure gleams of heavenly light,
Shall brighten all the skies.

" At evening time there shall be light."
If sorrow's hand should bear
Cold on our hearts, and draw her shroud
O'er what we hold most dear ;
Though sunshine, with each charm it brings,
May seem forever fled ;
Light, from Heaven's own celestial springs,
Shall rest upon our head.

" At evening time there shall be light."
Oh ! promise ever sweet
To those, who tread an unknown way,
With faint and faltering feet ;

They need not fear the coming hours,
  When sunset shall be past,
Since One, who knows that pathway well,
  Has promised light at last.

SPRING AND AUTUMN.

A little dust to overweep."

MRS. BROWNING.

Utterly, utterly out of our life,
  Already, each trace of his life is gone;
Only, sometimes, in the quiet eve,
  We stand, with a sigh, by the sculptured stone,
Which tells us the form we used to greet,
Dust amid dust, lies low at our feet.

Bright came the spring with sun and shower,
  The wood paths smiled in their vernal green;
To-day we have trodden the emerald grass,
  And wandered beneath the leafy screen;—
He welcomed the summer's early bloom;—
Now, it can only brighten his tomb.

Sigh, O leaves, on your rustling boughs,
  Even amid your smiling, sigh!
Did he not love your changeful charms?
  Yet, 'mid them all, he lay down to die.
Ye, in beauty, survive to-day,
A little while, ere ye pass away

The snow will come, and, with silvery veil,
  Wrap the earth for its winter's rest;
Before the flowers of the spring awake,
  We, like him, may sleep on its breast;
Time will each beauty of spring restore;
Only life's flowers return no more.

THE NIGHT COMETH.

Work! for the night is coming;
Work! through the morning hours;
Work! while the dew is sparkling;
Work! 'mid the springing flowers;
Work! while the day grows brighter,
Under the glowing sun;
Work! for the night is coming,
Night—when man's work is done.

Work! for the night is coming;
Work! through the sunny noon,
Fill the bright hours with labour;
Rest cometh sure and soon.
Give to each flying minute
Something to keep in store;
Work! for the night is coming;
Night—when man works no more.

Work! for the night is coming;
  Under the sunset skies,
While their bright tints are glowing,
  Work, for the daylight flies.
Work! till the last beam fadeth,
  Fadeth to shine no more;—
Work! while the night is darkening,—
  Night, when man's work is o'er.

THE DYING SUMMER.

Gently, sadly, the summer is dying—
  Under the shivering, trembling boughs,
With a low soft moan, the breeze is flying;
The breeze, that was once so fresh and sweet,
Is passing as swift as Time's hurrying feet,
And where the withered roses are lying,
The beautiful summer is surely dying.

Gently, sadly, the waves are sighing,
  The leaves are mourning that they must fall;
And the plaintive waters keep replying,

They miss the light that has decked them long ;
They have caught the last bird's farewell song ;
And lowly they murmur, from day to day,
" The beautiful summer is passing away."

Gently, sadly, the moon reclining
  High on her throne of azure and gold,
With wan clear light, o'er the world is shining ;
Wherever she turns there are teardrops shed,
They will gleam, till the chilly morn is breaking,
And the flowers with their last pale smiles are waking.

Wildly, sadly, the night winds swelling,
  Chants a measure wierd and strange,
Hark ! of the coming storm he is telling,
And the trembling life, that was almost gone,
Flickers and shrinks at the dreaded tone,
And scarcely lingers where, lowly lying,
The tender and beautiful summer is dying.

DEAD.

To live in hearts we leave behind
Is not to die!
CAMPBELL.

Dead? no! thou'rt living yet—
For while fond memory holds thee thus,
And love, we give not to the dead,
Is thine, thou still art one of us;
Not dead, till we forget.

Living, but far away;
Distance divides our hearts from thee—
But Time shall bring thee here again,
And brighter than all dreams, shall be
That one glad meeting day.

Alas! not so, thou'rt dead!
For it was sadly dear to me
To think thy spirit might be near;
From Earth's restraining-bands set free,
Yet here, by memory led.

“ Sweet could our hearts be known
Now, by some keener sympathy.”
Such my first thoughts when thou wert gone—
But soon the fancy ceased to be,
We felt thy soul was flown.

Dead ? no ! thou'rt living yet—
Distant, but we *shall* meet again,
And heart be read by faithful heart,
When love more closely draws his chain,
Round friends forever met.

PRECIOUS HOURS.

Treasure the hour of joy—
Welcome each draught of bliss, each golden dream ;
Find, if thou canst, beside life's bitter stream,
Pleasures without alloy;
But ever let thy heart's deep homage be,
Amid thy gladness, His, who gave it thee.

Treasure the time of grief—
Weep if thou wilt, but in that darker day
The humbled spirit sweetly learns to say,
"God giveth glad relief."
And sorrow dearer far than joy shall be,
If it but bring thy God more near to thee.

Treasure the hour of prayer—
There, seek from God food for thy hungry soul,
Full, and rich store ; no scant, penurious dole
Shall ever meet thee there.
Put by earth's sparkling cup of false delight,
And drink from Heaven's own chalice, life and light.

THE LAST RAY OF SUNLIGHT.

The last ray of sunlight! It gleams on the mountain,
  It gilds the dark pines in the valley below,
It blesses the flowers ere they sink to their slumbers,
  And the crystal brook catches its fugitive glow;
Never more lovely the sun's noontide glory,
  Never more lovely the first blush of morn,
Nor moonbeams, oft honoured in song and in story,
  Nor bright gleaming star in the still midnight born.

Hast thou e'er found a flower, whose frail stem has been broken,
  A fair blossom cast on the cold ground to die,
Its petals yet stainless, though life hath departed,
  Still smiling and bright, though its pride hath gone by?
Oh, like the smile and the perfume that lingers
  Decking the rude couch, where lowly it lies,
Latest defying the work of Time's fingers,
  Is the last ray of sunshine that brightens the skies.

The last ray of sunlight! It tells of the hours
  Gone from us forever and joined to the past,
And bids us remember the joys and the sorrows,
  Like sunshine and clouds, o'er our journeyings cast,

While in its brightness a promise is given,
Hopeful and dear, of a dawning to come,
And it beams on the heart, whose strong ties have been riven,
Like the welcoming light from the traveller's home.

AUTUMN.

Oh, tell me not of Autumn's charms,
The last sad beauties of the year;
Praise not the colouring of the leaf,
That is so dead and sere.

Give me the sunny hours of Spring,
Or Summer's rich, luxuriant store;
The opening bud, the blooming flower
That springs to life once more.

The stormy winds are whistling shrill
Among the branches in the wood,
And wrestling with the giant trees
That many a storm withstood.

They tear the creepers from the wall,
They lay our garden treasures low,
And bear a thousand lovely things
Far from us, as they go.

I shudder to my inmost heart,
To hear the bitter blast sweep by,
And think of frail and shivering forms
Beneath this wintry sky;

Of childhood and of helpless age,
That begs its bread from door to door
Amid this Autumn's tempest's rage;
God shield the homeless poor!

THE SECOND ADVENT.

In the hush of the silent midnight
Shall the cry of His coming be?
When the day of the Lord's appearing
Shall flash over earth and sea?

Shall it be at the morn's awaking,
And the beams of the golden sun
Grow pale and be quenched for ever,
When his journey is just begun?

We know not, we guess not, the hour;
But we know that the time must be,
When earth, with its clouds and shadows,
Will shrink, and tremble, and flee;

Will shrink to its deepest centre,
  And render before His throne,
The jewels the Lord will gather,
  The gems that He calls his own.

Then, bright in Heaven's noonday splendour,
  And robed like the dazzling snow,
The saints to their many mansions,
  The chosen and blest, shall go.

And songs of angelic gladness
  Be borne on celestial air
To welcome the mighty gathering,
  The throng, that shall enter there.

And, oh! in that awful parting,
  That day of unchanging doom,
When earth shall give up her millions,
  And empty her every tomb,

May we find in the Judge, a Saviour,
  A friend, whom we know and love,
And be bidden by Him to enter
  The courts of His house above.

CHRISTMAS SONG.

Go, bring me boughs of holly
  To deck the walls to-night,
Choose where the leaves are glossy,
  And the scarlet berries bright;
And bring the trailing ivy
  That by the oak doth grow,
And a bonny branch of the Christmas Tree,
  The charmèd mistletoe.

The holly by the windows
  Our sentinel shall be,
And the changeless ivy symbol
  Our love and unity;
Nor the flowers we prize be wanting,
  But high above their glow
We'll hang the branch of the magic tree,
  The charmèd mistletoe.

We gladly greet the holly,
  All thorny though it be,
And the dark and glossy ivy
  Will grace our revelry;
But many a bright eye sparkles,
  And many a cheek doth glow,
Beneath the spell of the magic tree,
  The charmèd mistletoe.

CHRISTMAS CAROL.

Two children singing in the street
With plaintive voices, low and sweet,
A simple strain, so soft and clear,
That many a passer stayed to hear,
And smiled or sighed to note their rhyme
In honour of the Christmas time.

" We are wanderers, wanderers ever,
  No friends, no home have we,
We sleep beside the river,
  Or 'neath the spreading tree ;
We have no kindred faces
  Our winter days to cheer,
Yet, we wish you a merry Christmas,
  And a prosperous New Year !

We see, through many a window,
  The gleaming firelight shine,
Shine on us, poor and friendless,
  Yet why should we repine ?
We know that He who seeth
  The poor, our cry will hear,
So we wish you a merry Christmas,
  And a prosperous New Year !"

PART II.

Miscellaneous Poems.

"Thus while I ape the measure wild
Of tales that charmed me, yet a child,
Rude though they be, still with the chime
Return the thoughts of early time,
And feelings roused in life's first day
Glow in the line and prompt the lay."

SCOTT.

Miscellaneous Poems.

IANTHE.

"Ianthe, golden haired!
Bright Hebe, in the glory and the bloom
Of her immortal youth, was not more fair
Than thou, O loveliest! when the slender boughs
Bent o'er thee, with their light leaves to caress
Thy long bright tresses—when upon the hill
Thy song resounded, and the joyous birds
Stopped their sweet warblings, but to learn of thee.
The river, when thy white and glancing feet
Pressed its smooth pebbles, played around thy form
In brighter eddies, with a murmuring song,
Such as young mothers sing above their babes,
But now, we miss thee on the mountain slopes,
And in the hamlets, and beside the stream;
Fairest and best beloved! return, return!"

So sang they in the valleys where they dwelt,
The white-browed daughters of that sunny isle,—
And Echo sadly gave the burden back,
Echo alone—and sighed, "Return, return!"
But never more, beside the forest shade,
Or rocky beach, at evening's calmest hour,
They railed thy form, Ianthe, brightest maid,
Or caught the silvery murmurs of thy song.

'Twas in a year long past, when summer days
Had waned in cloudless glory to the prime
Of vintage and luxuriant harvest fields,
When darkly o'er the heavens swept up the clouds
Hiding the sunlight, and, for many days,
Shrouding the isle in darkness. All around
The great sea-billows raised their foam-white crests
And dashed them on the beach with angry roar,
While the tall trees, upon the swelling hills,
Bent with strange gusts and howling savage winds.

The islesmen in wild terror sought the grove
Where holiest rites were done, and brought with them
Their costliest sacrifice and choicest gifts
To win the gods to mercy. All day long
The priest stood by the altar offering up
(It seemed so) vain prayers, vainer sacrifice,
Till suddenly at eve, on the fourth day,
There fell a blackness o'er the worshippers,
Darker than dark, and held them chained with awe;
Then through the cloud a voice, but what it said
None, not those nearest to the altar, heard
Save the priest only, and he answered low
With deep obeisance. Then the horror passed,
And light, such as there was before, returned.

From close beside the altar spoke the priest—
"Friends, seek your homes to-night; be sure of this,
The anger of the gods is not for nought,
Yet are they merciful—Even now, behold,
The sky grows clearer. At to-morrow's dawn
Assemble here once more,—then will I tell
Heaven's high behest, and see that ye obey."

Away into the vallies, sore amazed,
Passed the long train of people, and the night
Sunk down in calm and stillness, save that yet
The angry roaring waters rose and fell,
Boiling and surging round the beaten shore.

Morn came in glory, while the piled up clouds
In the far west yet spoke of danger near,
Forbidding fear to slumber—and with morn
Came to the temple, all the anxious throng,
Came with his stately step and flowing robe,
The venerable priest. Amid a hush
So deep they heard the stirring of the leaves,
He spoke to those around—" Friends, countrymen!
Consider what is dearest, what is best,
Of all our fair isle's treasures. Ask your hearts,
What holds the largest portion of their love?
And seek ye thus a stainless sacrifice,
For such the gods demand. Well know we all
We have too much forgotten in our wealth
The ever gracious givers, and have held

Our wives, our children and whatever else
We call our own, too much as being such ;
Wherefore the gods are angry, and command
Ere night return, we cast from yonder rock,
Into those fiercest waves, a gift of price
No less than is our eyes' most treasured light,
Our hopes' best stay, our ages' comforter,
Thus only, losing one, the best of all,
Can other lives of us and ours be saved,
Devoted else and doomed, with this our isle."

He ceased, and silence reigned, while glance met glance
In speechless questioning, and mothers strained
Their infants to their breasts, and fathers turned
To look into their fair young daughters' eyes
In trembling apprehension what would be
Next moment ; but next moment, every eye
Was turned on one, who stood there pale and calm,
Ianthe, daughter of the aged priest,
The fairest of the daughters of the isle.

Then passed a sudden shudder through the crowd ;
" Not thee, not thee, Ianthe," from each heart
Burst with a sudden anguish, but she stilled,
With one mute gesture, all the throng, and spoke :

" O father ! friends beloved ! if any be
Most fit to die in such a cause, 'tis I :
Thou knowest, Father, I have ever led
A simple innocent life, nor once have failed
To bring my daily offering to the gods
With prayers and due observance, from a child ;
Nor need I, friends, with gratitude repeat
How ye have ever blessed my glad, short life
With wealth of many hearts. I know full well
Ye will remember me with gentle thoughts,
And, best, will cheer my Father's lonely age
For his Ianthe's sake." She paused, and then
Turned to her sire and knelt, and prayed him bless
His child's resolve. He, who had meanwhile stood
Rigid as marble statue, and as pale,

Forced back with effort stern the agony
That gathered at his heart. He laid his hand
Untrembling on the locks of clustered gold
That hid his child's sweet face, and said, " 'Tis well :—
Well, dear Ianthe, hast thou said—and now
Thy Father gives thee, gladly, from his arms,
As thou hast given thyself."
Then, there arose
A sound of bitter weeping, and a wail
Of hopeless sorrow from the morn till noon,
And then a speechless awe. The eve drew on,
And sunset, when the dark and troubled sea
Must swallow up the jewel of the isle.

At last the hour was come. Upon the rock,
White robed and crowned with flowers, Ianthe stood;
Pale, with a glowing lustre in her eyes
Undimmed by fear or weeping. By her side,
Her father, wholly calm, except that still
His longing, loving gaze would follow her,
And tell the sickening anguish of his soul;

But yet he faltered not, and, as the sun
Went slowly downward to the glittering sea,
Glittering at rest far distant, slowly dropped
His eyes one moment on the billows near,
Then bade the maidens clustered round, commence
Their dedicating hymn. The strain arose
Softly and tremulous, then sunk again,
And rose once more, and would have quickly ceased
In tears and bursting sobs, but that one voice
Rose clear, and full, and sweet, and led them on ;
Thine, bright Ianthe ! Then the prayer was said,
And, 'mid an instant's pause of breathless pain,
She sprang, as springs the sea bird, from the height,
And the dark waters hid her evermore.

JOAN OF ARC.

PART FIRST.

A wild hillside beneath the winds of March—
With scattered sheep upon the tufted grass,
And here and there a tree, grotesque and lone,
Strong limbed, but stunted, like a sturdy dwarf
Misshapen, leafless. Overhead the clouds
Travelled with varying motion from the east;
Hurried, yet sullen; lagging on the breeze.

Up the rough path, that wound among the furze,
Slowly, with serious eyes that looked before,
(Her soul not seeing what their vision saw,)
With steps that knew the path too well to stray,
Moving, as habit, not as thought, ordained,
Came, through the chilly eve, a girl's slight form;
It was not till she gained the rounded brow,
Where east and north and south the hill sloped down
And showed the winding valley far below,
She turned and looked. Down there beneath her feet,
And sheltered by the huge arms of the hills,
Like a small nest amid the sturdy boughs

Whose well-tried strength defies the wildest storm,
The pleasant village, with its humble spire,
Lay calm and tranquil ; and the little streams,
Fed from the sunless caverns of the rocks,
Joining their slender threads of silver, ran
Through meadows, where a strip of level ground
Was bright with springing grass. A lovely scene
To stranger eyes, to hers 'twas more, 'twas home !
There, as she stood and looked, a sudden gust
Came right across the valley, bitter cold,—
She drew her mantle closer round her breast
And faced it boldly, while a vivid glow
Began to kindle in her soft, dark eye,
Gleamed like a beacon through a summer night,
Lighting her pallid cheek and thoughtful brow,
Till, with a sigh of smothered passion, broke,
From quivering lips—" Would I could die to save,
To save thee, O my country !—but I fear"—
So, with drooped eyes, she turned away and went
To seek her scattered flock and bring them home.

Clear from the village belfry rang the bell;
The gathered flocks, from mountain pastures led,
Were safely housed, and up the stony street
Came the small throng of evening worshippers.
Among them, with an old man by her side,
Came the pale shepherd girl, the dark-eyed Joan,
Of whom men said, she saw strange sights, and heard
Voices that others hear not. On they passed.
Soon rose the music of the evening prayer
Artlessly sweet, and floated to the skies
With sprinkled incense, on the darkening air.

The prayers were ended. Over each bowed head
The priest had poured his blessing; all were gone
But Joan, who yet before St. Catherine's shrine
Was kneeling, lost in prayer. Her fingers held
Her half told rosary, now all forgot,
Forgot the oft said words—her eager thoughts
Shaped themselves into fervid life and knocked
At heaven's high gate for entrance. By and by,
Her cheeks aglow, her frame with ardour thrilled,

She saw a dawning light break from the crown
That bound the saint's fair brow, and down it stole,
Enveloping the figure in a haze
Of golden splendour, while the sweet face wore
A heavenly smile, and from the carvèd lips
A soft voice uttered, "Joan, be strong of heart,
Take courage to fulfil thy own deep wish,
For thine it is to save thy native land."

Faded the smile, while yet the gazer bent
Her tear suffusèd eyes upon its beam—
Slowly the light died out, and nought was left
But her enraptured fancy echoing yet,
"Joan, it is thine to save thy native land."
Listening to this dear echo, long she knelt,
Till, through her dazzling dream, she faintly heard
A step upon the creaking belfry stair,
And the first note of curfew broke the spell.

Beneath the shadow of her father's roof
Joan passed and laid her down, but hours flew by
Ere sleep's soft pinions fanned her heated brain,
And when, at length, she slept, sweet dreams again
Repeated the sweet vision of the eve—
But not for long her slumber or her bliss.

When after midnight, scarce two hours were flown
Wild through the silence rang a fearful cry,
Then, swiftly following, shrieks, and oaths, and screams,
The tramp of horses, and the trumpet's blast,
While women shrieked, "They come! the spoilers come!"
And fled with wailing babes out through the night.

Happy were they who saved in that dread hour
Their lives and those they loved, although they stood
With Joan and that small household on the hill,
And watched the wreathing flames extend their arms
Till every dwelling shared the fell embrace,
A fearful sight—the sky glowed overhead,
And tenfold darker seemed th' abyss of night
Around those blazing walls, those ruined homes.

Darkly amid the glare, the old church tower
Showed the sad people that the house of God
Stood scatheless 'mid the wreck, but, oh! the cry
With they which marked the first red flame that twined
About the carving of the sacred door,
And, quickly spreading, mounted to the roof.

Kneeling upon the turf, with streaming hair,
With eyes of horror, and tight clasping hands,
Joan watched the burning rafters till they fell
And darkened the full glare of lurid light;
Then rose, and turning from the village, flung
Her arms about a young tree standing near
And hid her face upon them, while her heart
Cried out in her, "O God, deliver France!"
And made an answer to herself, and said,
"He will deliver us—a time will come,
Is coming quickly, to avenge our wrongs."

PART SECOND.

Now many days had passed since that dread time,
When midnight violence disturbed the night
To scatter death and ruin all around.
Back to their desolated homes again
The villagers had wandered from the hills
And desert places of their sudden flight.
Joan with her father came, and helped to raise
Some wretched shelter from the cold and storm,
Where they might light their household fires again.
  Darker and deeper since that awful hour,
Through days of misery when her heart was wrung
With sights and sounds of suffering, grew her thoughts.
Now ceaselessly she heard a voice that cried,
"Go forth, ordained of heaven, to save thy land!"
Strange visions visited her broken sleep,
And once, St. Catherine stood beside her bed
Divinely beautiful, in robes of light,
With grave, unsmiling brightness in her eyes.
Thus spoke she—"Wherefore dost thou linger here?

Thy country calls for thee, the promised maid,
Appointed by high Heaven to rescue France.
Rise, seek the King, for even now his mind
Is sore oppressed with evil. Tell him all—
And bid him greet the future as his friend,
For thou shalt stand beside him when the crown
Circles his brow in peace. Yet, if he need
Proof of thy mission, bid him quickly send
To where the holy fane of Firebois lifts
Its hoary head, and in a coffer old,
Dusty with age, and half by rust consumed,
There they shall find an ancient sword blade, marked
With three rude crosses. Let them bring it thee,
For by that weapon, and our Lady's help,
Thou shall recover France." So Joan awoke.
From thenceforth all her mind was set in her
To leave her village and her aged sire,
Travelling to seek the King: and weeks passed by
Slowly as years, until she found a time,
And, after many prayers and vigils kept,
Set forth upon her mission from her home.

PART THIRD.

'Twas a high day in Rheims—the sunlit streets
Were flooded full with life, and up and down
Rang the gay clangour of the burnished arms.
Pennons and scarfs and feathers waved in air,
And all of regal, all of martial state,
That France could muster, glittered round her King
For, now, the coronation oath was said,
And, now, the golden circlet, rich with gems,
With hallowing prayers, was placed upon his head.
Forth from the crowd uprose a joyous cry,
"Long live King Charles the Seventh!" uprose and swelled,
Over the swaying multitude around.

Bright through its space the vast cathedral gleamed
With arms, with beauty clothed in rich attire—
With priests in gorgeous vestments, mixed with men
In many a battle scarred—but near the King,
White robed above her glimmering suit of mail,
Holding a snowy banner in her hand,

And girded with her still victorious sword,
Stood the heroic maid, the prop of France.
Could this be she—the simple country girl,
Who watched her father's flock upon the hill
Or knelt among the village worshippers?
Had not this splendour changed her? for she stood,
Honoured among the nobles of the land,
Deliverer of her country in its need.
No! in the mournful paleness of her brow,
The strange, sad beauty of her clear brown eyes,
And firm, sweet mouth, still looked there forth the soul,
Once wrung with anguish for her country's woes,
And now, far looking onward to her own.

When all the rites were done, she slowly turned,
Kneeling before the King, and humbly spoke
" My liege, my work is done—when first I came
From my wild mountain home, and dared to stand,
I, a poor village girl, amid your court,
And promise boldly (what is now performed)

That this glad day should come, and through my help,
I but obeyed a loftier will than mine,
Inspired of Heaven to serve my country's need;
But now that need is past—my work is done—
Now let me go, back to my father's cot,
Back to my brother's dwelling—to my home!"

"Nay," said the King, "not so, we need thee still;
Thou, who hast led our troops to victory,
Shalt lead them yet, we cannot part with thee;
But meet it is, on such a day as this,
That we, such honour as a sovereign may,
So poor as we are, should bestow on thee,
Henceforth we make thee noble through all time;
Thou, and thy brothers, and thy aged sire,
And every one descended of thy line—
And, when our budding fortunes shall permit
Fit revenue to prop thy rank shall be
Added to honours. Wilt thou leave us now?
Well, then, if state and wealth can move thee not,
Listen, O maiden! to thy country's voice,

Still do the rude invaders tread her plains,
Still many a cruel deed of hideous war
Lays her fair dwellings waste. Return not yet!
She cries to thee, and Heaven will aid thee still.
He ceased. Before her sad and troubled eyes
What varying visions floated! but at last
She said—"I will not go," and sealed her doom.

PART FOURTH.

Another city, and another scene—
An ancient city, o'er whose pointed roofs
And many towers, perchance, the heavens were dark
With angry clouds and storms—perchance, the sun
Smiled in his brightness—what was it to her?
She only knew it was her day to die!

Through the barred windows, when the earliest dawn
Crept to her prison chamber, she was there
Kneeling before her little crucifix
Praying, until the murmured prayer was lost
In a wild rush of memory. Back they came
Her peaceful days of childhood—floated back
Her village home, the hillside, and the breeze,

And, strangely clear, the ringing of the bell.
Then, she was kneeling at St. Catherine's shrine,
Hearing again the silver tones that said,
"To thee is given to save thy native land."
And fancy bore her on from field to field,
From day to day of glory, till the last,
That highest hour of triumph, when she stood
Beside, while hoary prelates crowned the King.
Thence onward still, and still through victory,
But now no more she foremost—others came
And entered on her labours and her place.
And worse than all—the voices that had cheered—
The fearless faith in Heaven's high guidance—failed,
Doubts clustered round her, doubts of her own self
Tracking her footsteps darkly, till the night
Of blackest mis'ry when she knew herself
A prisoner, and deserted. "Woe to those,"
She cried aloud in bitterness, "who place
Their trust in princes! Was there not a knight
In all the noble army of the King
Could lift his arm for me, who saved the crown?"
Then weeping passionate tears, began again

Her broken prayers. So wore the early hours,
Till, by and by, her cruel jailers came,
And yet more cruel priests, who, with Christ's name
Upon their impious lips, could torture her,
That wretched woman, in her agony;
For now, no more sustained by lofty hopes,
Her spirit turned in anguish on itself,
Making wild conflict in her troubled breast,
Till at the last, when they had wrought their will,
And she, to save herself, with trembling hand
Had signed the dread confession of her crime,
Branding her memory with the double guilt
Of witchcraft, and denial of her faith,
They left her for a while, and in that hour
Peace came upon her soul and she was calm,
Looking for death as for a welcome guest.

At length they led her forth. Amid a crowd
Of thousands, as in other days, she moved;
Then, all was acclamation where she came,
Now, a dread silence reigned. The stake was reared
Amidst the open square, that all might see;

And many another goodly sight was there :
Princes and priests, rich-robed and gay with gems,
Knights in bright armour, and no lack of men,
Such as seemed human, come to look on her.
They bound her fast—she, scarce alive to thought,
Seeing them heap the faggots round her form,
Seeing the cruel faces of the throng,
No pity anywhere—grew cold as ice,
And shivered while she looked, not knowing why ;
So, in a trance of horror wrapped, she stood,
They deeming that she listened, while a monk
Told all her grievous sins aloud, and showed
In the great audience of the people there,
Her guilt and her confession. When he ceased
The fire was brought, and soon the kindled pile
Flaming around her, with rude shock called back
Each power of suffering. Then she wildly shrieked,
And, holding up her cherished crucifix,
Called upon Him, whose sacred form it bore,
Her last, sole refuge, for His pity then.
So the flame swept above her guiltless head,
And, with His name upon her lips, she died.

BOSCOBEL.

Half hidden in the circle of thy woods
Thou standest yet, unchanged and beautiful,
Thrice honoured relic of a famous time!
On History's page thou livest, but far more
In hearts that having loved thee, love thee still,
And keep thy smile in memory. On thy sward
The ever varying shadows dance and play,
And on thy grassy mound the daisies spring
New yearly, yet the same—the very flowers
Are blooming in thy quaint parterres that bloomed
Two hundred years ago.

I scarce can think
It was not yesterday the wanderer came—
That homeless wanderer—that uncrowned King—
Who, in his perilous and desperate plight,
Swayed England's loyal hearts with deeper power
Than when he held the sceptre—that he came
Seeking thy shades for safety. Then, all day,
The ceaseless summer rain that drenched thy boughs

Seemed weeping for the kingdom's downfall—He,
Meanwhile, must make his royal couch and throne
Beneath thy dripping leaves. Weary, oppressed,
Heartsick, and sad, by disappointment chilled
More than by wet or hunger, he must watch
The long hours through, nor dare to venture forth
Lest death be lingering near

Yet was he not
Deserted—there were noble hearts and true
Watching and labouring for their outcast King,
And, not the least among those honoured men,
Thy faithful band of brothers—still their name
Shall be the synonyme of gallant truth,
Unsullied honour, stainless loyalty.
Alas! that he to whom such faith was given
Proved so unworthy! that the promise bright,
He gave in danger and distress, should be
Like the white hoar frost on the morning grass,
And, when the sun of happier fortune rose,
Vanished in air. But that is nought to thee;
Thou, in thy leafy covert, art a shrine

Sacred to noblest virtues. Be thou still,
Time honoured spot! as sweet and fair as now;
No sacrilegious hand be ever raised
To mar with modern change thy ancient grace,
But be thou still, in tranquil beauty calm,
An ark of quiet 'mid life's changing scene;
And still, to generations yet unborn,
Repeat, in music, thy romantic tale.
Such scenes as thine, on England's verdant plains,
Make up her greatest charm, and dower her with
Matchless associations—for in her,
And in her hallowed shrines of bygone days,
We need not say, "Alas! for liberty!"
But liberty still lives, and, while we bless
With reverent love the good men of the past,
We proudly add, "Their spirit fires their sons,
And England's virtues, like her sturdy oaks,
Unhurt by age or storms, perennial spring."

HOME.

Oh, but one hour of solitude, to trace
Each well-known path, each childish hiding place!
Oh, but once more to see thee, and to know
Full liberty for farewell tears to flow!
What stranger faces gather round thy board?
What infant voices sound where ours were heard?
The flowers we planted, are they living yet?
Or passed their fragrance ere we could forget?
Some altered things in thee, I know full well,
But others, who that loved thee less, could tell?
Changes but slight, yet growing day by day
That steal insidiously thy charms away.
So years, that pass o'er some belovèd face,
The looks we loved, the smiles, may all efface,
May leave the outline as it was before,
Yet bid the loveliness return no more.
Oh, is it thus with thee? the trees are felled,
The trees, where twittering birds their counsels held.
But is the grass, where flickering shadows lay,
Still with the old familiar blossoms gay?

Ah! in dreams of thee, that stir my heart,
In vain I seek to see thee as thou art;
In memory's dwelling thou art painted fair,
And not a single change can enter there.
Thy different aspects, worn in many years,
All dear, all sanctified by smiles or tears,
Embalmed and treasured when their life was fled—
Immutable, as actions of the dead,
Dwell with me still, unalterably mine,
And fill, with incense of pure thoughts, their shrine.
'Tis strange, how in this arduous race of life,
Howe'er engrossing be the toil and strife,
Howe'er uncertain, wearisome and long,
Whatever rivals round our pathway throng,
Or when the goal approaches, and our eyes
Greet, bright, and almost won, the wished-for prize,
Still, half regretful, turn our thoughts again
To homes we left that glittering prize to gain,
Fondly recalling fireside pleasures fled,
And joys, o'er which long years a glory shed.

And if past days look bright when fortune smiles
Or proud ambition spreads her tempting wiles,
How fair they seem, when, baffled and distressed,
All that we ask is quietness and rest.

The traveller, journeying from the setting sun,
Turns to look back ere yet his toil is done,
And sees the hills, so steep and hard to climb,
All bathed in floods of rosy glory shine;
He sees the grassy slope, the sunny hue,
While distance hides the rocky path from view;
Forgets each dangerous step, each fatal snare,
And dreams that peace, alone, holds empire there.

So, could capricious wishes sway our life,
How oft from scenes with many a trouble rife,
Should we return to childhood's by-gone hours,
To find the roses vanished from the bowers!
To find that fancy, memory, love, had given
One half the charms that decked our ideal heaven;
To find that childhood hath its cares and fears,
Sad at the time, as those of after years;

And learn, too late, that all man's hours below,
Alike are chequered by the shades of woe.
Yet may we draw from nature's copious store
Of beauty, one similitude the more—
As the lone traveller when day is done,
And glowing clouds no more reflect the sun,
Sees from the distant ether o'er his head
One lovely star its silvery brightness shed,
And by and by the night that round him drew
So dark a veil is lit with splendours new,
That to his softened eyes seem scarce less fair
Than are the charms that daylight wont to wear,
So o'er the quiet days when life no more
Yields joy or pain so keen as those of yore,
A gentler light floats down upon our way
From stars unseen amid the beams of day.

A FOREST LEGEND.

Pleasant it was, when woods were green
  And winds were soft and low,
To lie amid some sylvan scene,
Where, the long arching boughs between,
Shadows soft, and sunlight sheen,
  Alternate come and go.

LONGFELLOW.

It was a summer morning,
  When dew lay on the flowers,
And birds sent up their joyous hymns
  From all the sylvan bowers,
I sat beneath an aged oak
Whose spreading boughs the sunbeams broke
  And cast them at my feet
In shattered fragments, bright and sheen,
That glittered on the mossy green,
Like splendid tints in prisms seen
  Where transient glories meet.

Clear mirror of the sky's deep blue,
  A stream went murmuring by,
And, where the grass luxuriant grew,
  It trickled dreamily;
And while its waters seemed to rest
On the wide mead's enamelled breast,
  The voices of the wood
Brought elfin music to my ears;
They seemed to sing of bygone years,
  And giant trees, that stood
Unaltered by the march of Time,
Through surly Winter's frost and rime,
  And Summer's gentlest mood,
Joined their deep notes to swell the strain,
And waved their branches o'er the plain.

The words they sang I cannot tell,
The fitful measure rose and fell,
Each fall and cadence, tone and swell,
  Mysteriously sweet,

Until the sun crept up unseen,
And noon beams fell upon the green
  That spread around my seat;
Then, sleep came o'er me, like a cloud,
And wrapped me in her silver shroud;
  When, to my slumbering ear,
A soft low voice the stillness broke,
And, as some finer sense awoke,
Sleeping, I heard each word it spoke,
  All measured sweet and clear:

"A thousand times the sun has called
  The young leaves from the tree;
A thousand times at winter's touch
  I've watched their verdure flee;
A thousand shoots to life have sprung,
A thousand birds their carols sung
  And filled the woods with sound;
Succeeding years roll slowly by,
The bright flowers blossom, fade and die,
Change is on all things, yet am I
  In changeless durance bound.

When first I woke, as from a dream
  How balmy seemed the air!
Forest and greensward, sky and stream,
  How exquisitely fair!
I loved the spot, the fragile stem,
Entrusted to my care,
I tended it with loving hand,
I watched each infant bud expand,
  Each tender leaf appear,
And still, as day by day it grew,
I gathered morning's choicest dew,
And wooed the freshest breeze that blew
  To scatter perfume here.

So time passed on, the slender stem
  Became a stately tree,
Whose branches, vigorous and green,
  Looked far o'er dale and lea;
Yon idle brook that creeps along,
Flowed then, a current wide and strong,
  Oft in whose shining face

The boar's fierce eyes reflected glowed,
Or antlered deer his beauty showed,
Bent o'er the waters as it flowed
  In still unconscious grace.

No human voice had e'er disturbed
  The calm that reigned around,
The shyest birds forgot to fear
  On this untrodden ground;
The squirrel leaped from tree to tree,
The fieldmouse ran, the labouring bee
Here garnered up his store;
The doves cooed softly to their young,
The nightingale her ditty sung,
The firefly's gleams all night were flung
  Trees, flowers, and streamlet o'er.

One day, strange sounds were in the wood,
  Strange sounds unheard till now,
The tread of horses, joyous tones,
  And laughter, clear and low;

A group emerging from the shade
Passed lightly down the open glade,
And paused beside the stream,
While nodding plumes waved in the air,
And sunbeams glanced on jewels fair,
Or on bright locks of waving hair
Cast many a golden gleam.

Brave steeds with goodly trappings gay,
And men of gallant mien,
And dames, whose mettled palfreys moved
Obedient to the rein;
It was a lovely sight to see,
And pleasant were the sounds of glee
That floated on the air;
They lingered here till dewy eve,
And e'en departing, seemed to grieve
A spot so beautiful to leave,
Where all things were so fair.

Silence, again, and loneliness
  Stole o'er the shadowy wood,
The shy deer's footsteps pressed the sward,
  Where those bright dames had stood.
Oh, were the hush unbroken still!
Unknowing then, of pain or ill
  My life had passed away;
Then, racking care, unbidden guest,
Had never filled my hapless breast,
Unknown had been this sad unrest,
  That mocks me day by day.

How did the seasons pass? I know
  Their changes oft went by.
I see them like the fleecy clouds
  In morning skies that lie;
A while, before the sun appears
To dry the golden may-flower's tears,
  All glorious they shine;
But soon, before his glowing light,
They pale and vanish from the sight,
Or robed, as erst, in tintless white,
  Lose all their hues divine.

Enough—they passed,—a sudden change
Came with one budding spring;
A bright, undreamed of, glowing life
Bathed every senseless thing;
Brightened the sunlight, and more fair
Painted each blossom, filled the air
With many a varying strain;
Woodsongs the quivering leaves that thrill,
Chords that the hush of midnight fill,
Tones from the falling of the rill,
The dropping of the rain.

Those summer days! those summer nights!
Not like the years before;
As long as thought and life remains,
I'll dream them o'er and o'er.
Too soon, the autumn breeze swept by
And darkened all my sunny sky;
Too soon, that transient light
Passed, like those northern gleams that throw,
When all the hills are white with snow,
O'er earth and sky their rainbow glow,
Yet fade and leave it night.

No more—within my narrow bounds,
  As I have dwelt, I dwell;
No change comes o'er the dreary life
  That once I loved so well,
Awake, O sleeper! for I hear,
From yonder covert, sweet and clear,
  The nightingale's first lay;
Go! and all spirits fair and bright
Keep thee in peace by day and night;
As thou dost tell the tale aright,
  Which thou hast heard to-day.

A BALLAD.

"Mother! open the door,
The wind blows chilly and bleak;
Mother! open the door,
For I'm growing faint and weak."
Up she rose from the fire,
Rose up from her lonely watch,
Quickly she went to the door,
And quickly lifted the latch.

Out she looked on the night,
The wind blew bitter and shrill,
But nothing there could she see,
And the voice she had heard was still;
Back, with a heavy sigh,
She went to her fireside seat,
But the voice was there once more,
And the sound of childish feet.

She leaned her over the bed,
  Her lips were parched and blue,
The eyes of the dying were open wide
  And she saw that he heard it too.
His eyes were open wide
  With a ghastly look of dread,
And, when she had watched him a moment's space,
  She turned away from the dead!

She opened the door again
  And looked out through the tempest wild,
And she thought she saw, at the forest side,
  The form of a little child.
With a cry of anguish and fear,
  She rushed to where it stood,
But its garments were gleaming farther on
  In the darkness of the wood.

Still, she followed it fast,
  And still, it flitted before,
Until she thought her weary limbs
  Would bear her on no more;

Still, as the night wore on,
She followed the flying shade,
Till she came to an old stone carvèd cross,
And there knelt down and prayed.

There, with a breaking heart,
She prayed to be cleansed within ;
That her mind might be freed from its deadly chain.
And her soul be washed from sin.
She prayed till the light was faint
In the east, when a slumber stole
Over her weary senses,
Soothing her guilty soul.

The trees were dripping above her,
The skies were stormy and wild,
But she saw nought in her slumber,
Save the form of a little child.
The child stood close beside her,
And spoke in accents low,
Not like the tones of terror,
That haunted her, hours ago.

"Mother, here in the forest
  You left me to starve and die,
And here, where my bones are bleaching,
  Your lifeless corpse must lie;
But now, the gates of Heaven
  May open to let you in,
For true and hearty repentance
  Has washed away your sin."

Up rose the sun in his glory
  And lighted the forest glade,
And shone on the old stone cross,
  Where the woman's form was laid;
The grass grew high around her
  Heavy with dew and rain,
But she lay wrapped in a slumber
  That never knew waking again.

PENELOPE.

The palace halls were hushed, where late the voice
Of boisterous feasting through their columns rung.
Silence, without, her viewless wing did poise,
And Night on high her starry banner hung:
Upon the meadow slopes the waves were flung
With slumberous murmur, as they rose and fell;
And drowsily, from shadowy groves among,
Came now and then, to mingle with their swell,
Faint sounds, that seemed of neighb'ring flocks and herds to
tell.

One chamber there, with kindly step and slow,
Sleep entered not through all the lonely night;
But hour by hour, the torch's ruddy glow,
O'er a wife's vigil, shed its dusky light.
Not yet, by time was bowed her stately height,
Nor harshly touched her queenly brow by care,
Yet wept she for the years of past delight
And dreaded sorrows, that she yet must bear,
While rose, with tears, to Heaven, her oft repeated prayer.

"Dread King of Ocean! on thy wild domain
See'st thou my wanderer's bark, too long delayed?
Upon some treacherous rocks doth it remain?
Or hath it near some pleasant isle been stayed?
Pity, oh pity thou, my heart's long pain
And yield him to his home, in peace again.

And thou, whom all the worshipped gods above
He most has honoured, deign to be his guide!
Goddess serene! restore him to my love,
And o'er his varying fortunes still preside;
Oh, guard him till, his weary wanderings o'er,
Again I greet him on his native shore.

And, since my years must pass without his care,
Who wont to shield me from each breath of ill,
Let thy benignant spirit hover hear,
And keep my heart and life unsullied still;
Hard is my task to hold the trust he gave,
But thou, in each distress, canst guide and save."

Her accents ceased, her bowed head drooping low,
  O'ermastered by the flood of love and grief;
No longer could her thoughts in language flow,
  But heavy tears fell fast,—a sad relief;
  Before her heart's clear vision rose the Chief
As when she saw him last in manhood's prime,
  So lifelike—for one moment, bright and brief,
She smiled, but no! he trod a distant clime,
And she must weep alone, and chide the lingering time.

THE SIEGE.

There was of old a maiden citadel,
  And for it two great powers contested long;
Humility besieged—so legends tell,
  But Pride still held the inner fortress strong;
Humility had gained the outer wall,
And hung his banners there, but that was all.

But after a long time, a stranger came
  To the besieger's camp, and promised aid.
His name was Love, a strategist of fame,
  And many were the conquests he had made;
He travelled in a low and simple guise,
And Pride might well such power as his despise.

Love went to work with mining tools, and sought
  A passage through the living rock below;
Day after day, and hour by hour, he wrought
  With hopeful progress still, albeit slow;
At length he found a low, unguarded cave,
That to the inner fortress entrance gave.

Then he and that great chief, Humility,
  Together entered by the secret way;
And Pride, who dreamt not of defeat so nigh,
  Fled from his high command in sore dismay;
So peace was made within; but from that hour
Humility and Love held equal power.

IMOGEN.

"Ere I could tell him
How I would think on him at certain hours
Such thoughts, and such."

CYMBELINE.

Fall gently, gently, shades of night!
Rise up, sweet moon, o'er hill and dale,
And shed from yonder tree-crowned height
Your silver radiance, pure and pale.

Blow on, soft breeze, and bear away
The idle words that pain my ear;
The jarring voices of the day,
A little while, I need not hear.

Now all is still—the fresh, calm air
Brings me the fragrant souls of flowers;
Ah! would, my love, that it could bear,
At least, a messenger from ours.

Vain fancy! yet I need but sleep
  And straight behold thee in my dream,
Pictured on mem'ry's mirror deep,
  Clear as the heavens on Severn's stream.

For when cold Reason yields her reign,
  And outward sense lies dead and still,
Love opes the portals of the brain,
  And ushers in the guest he will.

Good night, dear love, thou too mayst hail
  The breathing of these zephyrs light;
Oh, fly to greet him, gentle gale,
  And whisper low, Good night—good night!

WOMEN'S RIGHTS.

You cannot rob us of the rights we cherish,
  Nor turn our thoughts away
From the bright picture of a "Woman's Mission"
  Our hearts pourtray.

We claim to dwell, in quiet and seclusion,
  Beneath the household roof,—
From the great world's harsh strife, and jarring voices,
  To stand aloof ;—

Not in a dreamy and inane abstraction
  To sleep our life away,
But, gathering up the brightness of home sunshine,
  To deck our way.

As humble plants by country hedgerows growing,
  That treasure up the rain,
And yield in odours, ere the day's declining,
  The gift again ;

So let us, unobtrusive and unnoticed,
  But happy none the less,
Be privileged to fill the air around us
  With happiness ;

To live, unknown beyond the cherished circle
Which we can bless and aid;
To die, and not a heart that does not love us
Know where we're laid.

A WAR SONG.

Loud peals the trumpet through the land, o'er city and o'er plain,
And wakes each echo of the hills again, and yet again!
A thousand dauntless hearts arise, a thousand voices blend
From far and near with one accord, a glad response to send.

"We come, as erst our fathers came, and He whose mighty power
Was with them, shall protect our arms in battle's fearful hour;
The stainless honour they bequeathed unsullied shall remain,
And in His might, the cause of Right our good swords shall maintain."

Arise! O Lord of Hosts, arise! our strength and helper be;
Go forth before our armies and give them victory;
So shall they to their native land return with glory crowned,
And through old England's borders fair Thy praises shall resound.

Alas! a darker shadow falls upon our spirits now;
Grief swells in many a heart to-day and sits on many a brow;
The mother, by her lonely hearth, prays for her children dear,
The maiden weeps within her bower in anguish and in fear.

Of all the loving and the loved who part from us to-day,
We know that some are marked for Death, his earliest noblest prey;
But who can read the fatal sign? what quick perception trace
The growing shadow of the tomb on some familiar face?

Away with such desponding thoughts! our parting words should be
Such as may echo through their hearts when flushed with victory,—
Such as, if memory brings them back in peril or in pain
Gleams from the sacred light of home, their power may still retain.

ALMA.

There comes a murmur o'er the sea of mingled joy and woe,
From where, O Alma! stained with blood, thy rapid waters flow;
The shout of triumph blends with sobs of anguish, stern and deep,
Yet love and pride have mighty power to comfort those who weep.

And we, who, wand'ring far from home, in distant lands abide,
Forget not those who on thy banks have nobly fought and died;
The hope and flower of each fair land together, foes no more,
Brothers in death lie side by side, upon thy fated shore.

The laurels, planted in our hearts and watered by our tears,
Shall live to mark their honoured graves through many passing years;
And though the land in darkness lie their resting place around,
Yet, where they sleep—the brave and free—is consecrated ground.

Rejoice, O England! 'mid thy tears, rejoice to hear it told
How well thy sons maintained the fame their fathers won of old;
To show the world that Peace may shed her blessings o'er the land,
Nor weaken one courageous heart, nor rear one feeble hand.

And thou, fair France! e'en by the bier where sleeps thy gallant chief,
Let joy and exultation find a place amid thy grief;
Nobly he fills a soldier's grave, although not in the strife,
But worn by sickness long endured, he yielded up his life.

Oh, may the memory of the hearts grown cold by Alma's shore,
Draw closer yet the bands of love between us evermore;
England and France, together joined, resistless in the fight,
May conquer still for those oppressed, may still defend the right.

LINES TO A FRIEND.

MARCH, 1859.

I would have had you see to-day, my friend,
How beauteously our Canada can vie
With our still dearer England, in the charm
Of sky and lake and river. Here no fields,
Here, in this western wilderness afar,
With soft rich verdure, rest the grateful eye,
But, on a day like this, we think no more
Of what *would* please us, but of what *does* please.

The sky was cloudless; of that loveliest blue
Not dark, but like the bright forget-me-not,
That jewel of the hedgerows—with a clear,
Soft, pure transparence, the best gift of spring.
And then our river! oft, I love to watch
Its dancing, rippling waters, and to-day
They had an added dower of loveliness.
All over its bright surface, deeply blue,
Glittered and sparkled with a thousand rays,
Gems, coronals, and chains of broken ice.

I could have dreamt, the genii of the lamp
Had heaped the waters with the costly freight
Of jewels, for Aladdin's matchless pile.
Long stood I on the shore, and could not tear
My feasted eyes from such a lovely scene,
Till the clear waters 'gan be tinged with gold,
And, slowly, slowly, westward sank the sun.

Then what a glory crested every wave!
And every gem, that shone and gleamed before,
Shot forth a million sparks of coloured flame,
Crimson and green and blue. Beyond, the pines,
Far off, against th' horizon, let the light
Break through them in long, level rays, and showed
Like a dark network on the glowing sky.
High in the heavens some clouds—I know not whence
They came, for just before there was not one—
Majestically floated, robed in hues
Of matchless beauty. Those that highest lay
Were tinted with that pure and delicate green
You've seen on pearl-like sea shells, with an edge
Of softly shaded rose. A lower tier,

In rich resplendent gold and purple, shone,
And all above, around, below, the hue
Of the clear ether gradually changed
From loveliest azure, to the deepest tints
Of glowing crimson.
Ah! but what avail
My feeble words to tell what never yet
The highest genius called to perfect life
Upon his canvas? Yet 'tis not in vain
That I have tried to reproduce for thee
The scene I loved to look on—not in vain.
For writing thus, I, in my thought, have heard
Again the voice that spoke from stream and sky
Silently eloquent, and said, "Behold
The glory of God's footstool! What must be
The brightness of His throne? To Him then raise
Thy wonder and thy worship evermore."

THE BALLAD SINGER.

It was a street, where still, from morn till eve,
Flowed on the living tide with ceaseless swell;
A thousand different faces passed it by,
A thousand different footsteps trod its stones,
But, ever as they came, they seemed to bear
On wrinkled brows and in their restless eyes,
The seal that stamps the votaries of wealth.
So passed they daily—it had been as strange
To see, amid that dry and trodden way,
A rose tree in luxuriant wealth of bloom,
As there to meet a face, untouched by care.
One day, the busiest passers caught a sound
Unwonted there—"What is it?" "Oh! pass on,"
'Tis but a ballad singer." Yet that voice
Clearly harmonious, heard above the din,
As though those silver notes were all too pure
To mix with baser sounds, had some strange charm,
And stayed some hasty steps—'Twas thus she sung:

I am blind, and the light is gone,
Forever, is gone from me,
I dwell in the city alone,
I wander its pathways of stone,
Yet ever I seem to see
A beautiful home, where the sun shines bright,
All rich in the beauty of verdure and light.

There's a tree by the garden gate
Where the birds sing all day long,
And a seat, where they often wait
When the tranquil eve grows late
For the nightingale's lovelier song,
And beyond, a meadow slopes gently away,
Where they hear the laugh of the children at play.

There peeps from the windows bright
A spirit of heartfelt joy,
And winter and summer, and day and night,
It blesses the household with calm delight,
And pleasures that never cloy;
'Tis the pure home love that hallows the spot,
And sheds its light o'er that peaceful cot.

THE ISLANDER'S SONG OF HOME.

Oh, give me back my home!
Brightly may shine
The land to which we roam—
It is not mine.

Give me the hills again!
The glorious hills,
Whose fragrant breath the soul
With rapture fills.

Give me the sounding sea!
Its hollow roar,
Dear beyond words to me,
Give me once more.

I wake amid the night,
All is so still;
Oh! could its murmured voice
The silence fill!

Or dreaming, I behold
The tall ships glide,
With white and tapering masts,
O'er the blue tide.

These are the sights I see
Where'er I roam;
Nought has such charms for me—
Give me my home!

CLARISSA HARLOWE.

A SMALL PICTURE, BY LANDSEER, IN THE VERNON COLLECTION.

Last seen in old England's sunlight, how well I recall it still,
With the sense of a present pleasure, responding to memory's
thrill;
Yet, 'tis but a simple picture, a sordid and squalid room,
Enclosing a single jewel, a girl in her girlhood's bloom;

Not in the pride of beauty, decked with joy's radiance fair,
But worn by a thousand terrors, bending in humble prayer;
The flaring light by the chimney, the bed that no form has prest,
Tell of her lonely watching, through the long hours of rest.

Perhaps, in the dark, dark midnight, there came but the voice
of fear,
Whispering of deadly peril, none but betrayers near:
How the chill hours crept o'er her, helpless, deceived, alone,
None but her own heart witnessed, none but herself have known.

None? Ere the first pale sunbeam shone through the dusty
pane,
Faith, with returning brightness, rose in her soul again;
Deep is the calm that follows when the loud storm is past—
After the night of anguish, Hope's daystar smiles at last.

Over the golden tresses, loosed from their shining bands,
Over the kneeling figure, over the clasping hands,
Over the sweet face downcast, over the patient brow,
Day's earliest light and purest pours through the casement
now.

Thus, after years of absence, vivid, and pure and bright,
She, in some hour of dreaming, rises before my sight;
Thus Art, with magic pencil, sketching a vision fair,
Preaches of faith and patience, faith that can quell despair.

THE RENEGADE.

> "He has thrown by his helmet and cross-handled sword,
> Renouncing his knighthood, denying his lord."
>
> SCOTT.

Ye bid me to the worship of my fathers to return;
Ye bid me from my side each sign of Moslem power to spurn;
But even should I kneel no more before each gorgeous shrine,
The faith, the trust of childhood, can never more be mine.

Can ye give me back th' untainted heart, the spirit free from guile?
The sleep that fell so gently, that parted with a smile?
No! sooner could the grave give up the friends, whose holy tears
Might wash, from my polluted soul, th' apostacy of years.

Once, I could kneel in simple faith, and breathe a heartfelt prayer;
But now, my heart is steeled and cold, nought holy dwelleth there;
I may look back with longing gaze, but never may retrace
The fatal steps that part from me each Christian name and race.

Torment me, then, no longer, for fain would I forget
The broken links, whose traces have power to pain me yet;
For me the wine-cup and the sword! for me war's crimson
state!
To offer other joys than these, thou com'st too late, too late!

THE PRINCE'S WELCOME.

Swift as the lightning's vivid flash
The welcome tidings come,
Forging another link to bind
Ours to our fathers' home.

Far spreading o'er our Western World,
O'er forest, lake, and hill,
"The Prince! at length the Prince is come!"
Thus runs the message still.

From those far-stretching wave-worn coasts,
Where ocean billows roar,
To where St. Lawrence' gathered floods
Their mighty torrents pour;

Where, o'er the bright encircling wave,
Quebec's proud fortress stands,
And twines with mem'ries of the past
The present's glowing strands;

Where Commerce marks her favoured isle,
  And where, from side to side,
Marvel of man's creative skill,
  The bridge o'erspans the tide;

Thence, by Ontario's broad expanse,
  The magic signal flies;
And, with a welcome deep and true,
  The nation's heart replies.

The new-born cities of the West
  Are stirred with joyful haste,
For o'er the forest and the plain
  The joyful news has passed;

To this far realm, where Huron's flood,
  Still bears the bark canoe,
And still the hardy settler toils
  Primeval forests through.

Hark! where it comes the waiting crowds
  Break forth with glad acclaim,
That blends with his, the empire's hope,
  His mother's honoured name.

"For Her dear sake, to whom each heart
In loyal faith bows down;
For Her, who wears her people's love,
Best jewel of her crown;

For Her, our pride of womanhood,
A thousand hearts as one,
In this Her western empire, bid
Glad welcome to Her son!"

THE BRACELET.

Before a straw-thatched cottage,
Upon the white sea shore,
A woman with her busy wheel
Sat spinning by the door;
The sun went down upon the sea,
And shone with ruddy glow,
While the woman, to her humming wheel,
Sang dreamily and low:
"Oh, thus the busy world goes round,
Or joy or sorrow bringing;
And those it raises up to-day,
To-morrow, downward flinging."

All day the waves had murmured low
Scarce stirred by summer breeze,
And now the tide came rolling up
The wealth of distant seas;
It brought, upon its gathering foam,
Some waif that gem-like shone,
The woman heeded not, but still
Went softly singing on:
Oh, thus the busy world goes round,
Or joy or sorrow bringing;
And those it raises up to-day,
To-morrow, downward flinging.

But now, a level line of light
Shone broadly o'er the land,
And struck a thousand sparkles out
From something on the sand;
A jewelled clasp, a slender band,
That might have decked, erewhile,
A lovely lady's arm, and gleamed
Less lovely than her smile:
But thus the busy world goes round,
Or joy or sorrow bringing;
And those it raises up to-day,
To-morrow, downward flinging.

The woman checked her busy wheel,
And ceased her murmured song,
To glance a moment out to sea,
The rolling waves along,
Until the jewel caught her eye;
She raised it from the ground,
And softly rose her song again
Above the treasure found:
Oh, thus the busy world goes round,
Or joy or sorrow bringing;
And those it raises up to-day,
To-morrow, downward flinging.

ON SOME VIOLETS.

RECEIVED FROM ENGLAND, MARCH 1855.

The sunny hours of summer
More brilliant flowers may bring,
Their many coloured blossoms
O'er all the land may spring;

The pure and stately lily,
The bright imperial rose,
May bloom, yet pass unheeded by,
Ere winter's storm-wind blows;

But ye, fair faded flowers,
  Your day of beauty o'er,
Shall still be prized and cherished
  As dearly as before.

A thousand pleasant memories,
  A thousand thoughts of home,
From hidden corners of the heart,
  At your sweet summons come;

And, 'mid smiles and tears fast rising,
  We speak of days long past,
The season when we gathered
  Old England's spring-flowers last.

The maiden snowdrop, guarded
  By spear-like leaves around,
The starlike, golden crocus,
  That glitters on the ground;

We loved them well, and prized them,
  The first-born of the year,
But the early perfumed violets
  We ever held most dear;

Nestling in sheltered places,
  When the snow-wreaths melt away,
With dewy smiles receiving
  The warm sun's welcome ray.

Bright Hope and sunny Pleasure,
  Lurked in each tiny flower,
And still these withered blossoms
  Retain their heartfelt power.

They tell of kind remembrance,
  Of love, unchanged and true,
Of friendship, dearer to our hearts,
  Than rarest scent or hue.

EVENING.

Hushed is the thunder,
  The storm has passed by,
Floats not a raincloud
  Across the clear sky;
In the west lingers
  The glory of day,
Gleams on the mountains
  Its last golden ray.

In the dark forest
  The breeze is at rest,
Not a wave ruffles
  The lake's silver breast;
Gently the flowers
  Have sunk to repose,
Softly among them
  The rivulet flows.

One fair star beaming
  In radiance above,
Sheds o'er their slumbers
  The pure light of love;

Calm, serene, tender,
The aspect she wears,
Her smile celestial,
Shining through tears.

All the wide landscape
Lies silent and still,
No sound in the valley,
No voice on the hill;
Slowly the bright tints
Fade from the sky;
Risen in splendour
The moon floats on high.

Night in her beauty
Descends on the land;
Dewdrops are scattered
Like pearls from her hand;
O'er bird, tree, and flower
Her pure gifts she throws;
To man, worn and weary;
She giveth repose.

THE OLD WIFE.

Yes, she is old—she must be old,
For I remember long ago
Her tresses gleamed like living gold,
That now are white as drifted snow,
And the pure oval of her face,
The fair round cheek and sunny brow,
The pliant form's unrivalled grace
Have lost their early freshness now.

Old—yet believe it as you will,
The tender beauty fair and bright,
That stirs me in remembrance now,
As when I first beheld its light,
Was not, nor could be, half so dear,
As are the looks I meet to-day,
Where Time has given with every year,
More charms than e'er he stole away.

For in her face I love to read
The records of her faithful love,
My solace in each hour of need,
My anchor that no storm could move;
For me each day of care she bore,
For me and mine the tears she shed;
Remembr'ing all, I can but pour
A thousand blessings on her head.

SONG.

RESPECTFULLY DEDICATED TO THE

"WOMEN'S RIGHTS" CONVENTION.

Our husbands they may scold or snore,
Or bake, or fry, or stew;
While we this man-spoiled world restore,
And make it good as new.

* * * * * * *

No husband's mission own we now,
To bully or to bore;
"Obedience" of the marriage vow,
Shall form a part no more.

PUNCH.

Maid of France! whose armèd hand
Saved of old thy native land;
Lady! on thy castle wall
Aiding, cheering, leading all;
Ye, and hundred names beside
Shining through war's crimson tide,
Show that *we* can rule the fight,—
Show, command is Woman's Right!

Wit, her female votaries claims,
Learning guards their honoured names;
Art and Poetry have found
Women to their service bound;
History's voice aloud declares
Choicest gifts were ever theirs;
Why should *we* then wear the chain?
Let us have our Rights again!

Home affections! peaceful hours!
Fireside joys, that once were ours;
Vain delusions! meant to keep
Women's souls from loftier sweep,
We have cast you all away.
Husbands, children, what are they?
Ours no more each household task,
Injured Women's Rights we ask!

A PEEP AT THE FAIRIES.

Come out, come out of the stifling rooms,
Come out in the summer air;
The cool night winds blow over the fields,
The fragrant sweetbriar its perfume yields,
And the skies are bright and fair.

And see, oh see, o'er the smooth mown grass
The flickering lights that play;
Are they the firefly's lamps that gleam?
No! by the brightness of every beam,
The fairies keep holiday.

Now, for the roof of their festal hall,
A sweetbriar spray is bent;
And for curtains of tissue, silvery white,
Studded with wonderful pearls of light,
A spider his web has lent.

Yonder, two elves with all their might
Come dragging a mighty stone;
A pure white pebble, smooth and fair—
Now they have placed it, with heed and care,
'Tis surely meant for a throne!

What will they do for a canopy?
  Ingenious elves are they
See! they have hung a roseleaf sweet
Floating over the royal seat,
  Under the sweetbriar spray.

A large, smooth leaf from a laurel bough
  Some friendly wind has rent,
This shall their festal table be
Loaded with spoils of flower and bee,
  Laid 'neath the cobweb tent.

Hark! I hear from the thicket side
  The sound of a fairy horn,
Soft, as the dewdrops on the grass,
The trickling rills of music pass,
  On flitting breezes borne.

And now they come, in martial state
  Surrounding their tiny Queen:
Gentles and Dames, a courtly train—
And, marching in time to the minstrel strain,
  Come archers in garb of green.

All lit by the fairy torchlight's gleam
They wind o'er the dewy sod;
And the green blades spring from the pressure light,
And the uncrushed daisies glimmer white,
Where an instant past they trod.

No more must we gaze,—some hurtful spell
Still follows the curious eye;
And evil befalls the luckless wight,
Who dares in the starry summer night
Intrude on their revelry.

SONG.

Written for the Air entitled "Mary Astore."

Not when the summer days
Glide softly by;
Not when the lark's sweet lays
Float from the sky;
Not when bird, flower, and bee
Fill earth with melody,
Let one sad thought of me
Waken thy sigh.

And when the winter fire
    Sheds its clear light;
Just ere the year expire
    That rose so bright;
When laughter's silver sound
And the glad song goes round
Be no dark memory found
    Haunting the night.

But when the silent hour
    Of man's deep rest,
Bids memory's sleepless power
    Reign in thy breast,
Then, let the thought of me
Float through the air to thee,
And in thy visions be
    A welcome guest.

ITALY.

Phœnix of Nations! from the smould'ring heap
  Of ashes, whence thou spread'st thy radiant wing,
  How have we watched and joyed to see thee spring
In vigorous life, as one refreshed by sleep!
Now, smiles illume the eyes, that wont to weep,
  And blessings, from afar, are o'er thee shed,
  While Freedom's children greet thy crowned head.
We, from her island seat, amid the deep,
We, who have sorrowed for thy hour of pain,
  Now bid thee, on thy brightening way, "God speed!"
  May He, whose Spirit can alone make free,
Whose word hath called thee into life again,
Preserve thee evermore in every need,
  And twine the olive wreath of peace for thee.

GENIUS.

Envy not, thought of mine, those whose rich dower
Is genius, heaven's most dazzling gift to men ;
Admire, but envy not ; for oh ! to them,
Great is the peril wedded to the power.
Blest, trebly blest, if in each dangerous hour
  Religion guides them with her ray divine ;
  Then, on their kind, like Spring's sweet days they shine
With vivifying gifts of sun and shower ;
But awful is the might, and dread the doom,
  Of genius unennobled and unblest,
  Whose gleam is but the lightning's baleful ray,
Flashing with fatal splendour through the gloom,
Death-fraught and dying : let me rather rest
  Where on my sheltered path may beam the day.

THE MEADOW.

> And must this parting be our very last?
> No! I shall love thee still, when death itself is past!
> CAMPBELL.

The summer sun shone bright and clear upon the champaign
fair,
And incense of a thousand flowers perfumed the golden air;
The clover blooms bent down their heads beneath the lab'ring
bee,
And mother-birds, on tiny nests, peeped forth from bush and
tree.

The meadow land sloped gently down around the shining pool;
Tall were the rushes on its bank, its waters deep and cool;
There the gay foxglove reared her head in queenly pomp and
pride,
And sheltered, with her friendly leaves, the violets by her side.

Gems from Aurora's tresses flung, the diamond sparks of dew
Still glittered where the hedgerow trees their partial shadows
threw;
Beyond, the wood anemones their slender stems upbore,
And golden cowslips on the turf outspread their fragant store.

Along the path a wanderer came with weary steps and slow,
But, as she paused and looked around, her dim eyes seemed
to glow,
And once she bent to pluck the flowers that bloomed about her
feet,
Then, with a sudden pang, drew back, nor touched the blossoms sweet.

"No, not for me!" she inly sighed, "not for such hands as mine,
Ye lovely meadow flowers, it is your gentle charms to twine:
Ye are for childhood's happy hours, that know no touch of
care,
And innocent and loving hearts beat lightly where ye are.

"Why should a moment's sudden thought, a flash of memory,
bring
At once before my heart and eyes my childhood's vanished
spring?
Methought the flowers I gathered here, yes *here*, were blooming still,
And I could hear the busy hum of yon long silent mill.

"How sweet! how bitter! could it be that I might feel again
The child-heart beating in my breast, the child's pure life regain?
No! the sharp anguish of the thought that forced my touch away
From those pure flowers would still be near to haunt me night and day.

"I go, I go.—Between the days that I but now recall
And this dark present which infolds my spirit in its thrall,
These hands themselves have dug a gulf across whose depths untold
Too well I know I may not pass to breathe the peace of old.

Farewell, sweet blossoms! There are hours when e'en such hearts as mine
Are purified by holy sleep, and bathed in visions fine;
Then in my dreams I'll wander here, and then no thought shall stay,
But I will pluck your tender forms, and bear your charms away."

Above the flowery greensward she bent with tender grace,
As when a mother bends to kiss her child's fair sleeping face—
A mute caress without a touch—then through the summer day
Went like a shadow dark and sad, and slowly passed away.

RETROSPECTION.

'Tis not well to forget—it is good to recall
  As we bask in the sunshine, the storms that have been,
When the joy of the present shines bright over all,
  To remember a moment the darkness we've seen ;
For there was not a day when some light did not break
  Like an angel from heaven thro' the tempest's dark shroud,
And Hope with fresh smiles from her slumber awake,
  As the fair bow of promise shone bright on the cloud.
'Tis not well to forget,—in the night of the soul
  'Tis well that our visions should be of the past ;
Thus assured that the shadows asunder will roll,
  And leave us a morning as bright as the last ;
For the Hand that has guided, is guiding us still ;
  By the way that He led us, He leadeth us yet,
And sorrow's dark terrors, or pleasure's keen thrill,
  May whisper alike " 'Tis not well to forget."

ECHO SONG.

Ye Echoes of this lovely lake,
  Oh tell me if, returning never,
I shall again your answers wake ;
Say must my absence be forever ?
    Echo : Forever !

Ye trees, that here in beauty grow
  And look o'er vale and field and river,
Ye see me grieve that I must go ;
  But tell me will it be forever ?
    Echo : Forever !

Here dwell the early friends of youth,
  From whom no change my heart can sever;
Oh tell me, will they keep their truth,
  And do I leave them now forever ?
    Echo : Forever !

Then lovely scene, a long farewell !
  Again I tread thy margin never,
Too well my fate thine echoes tell,
  But I'll remember thee forever.
    Echo : Forever.

A SUMMER NIGHT.

Oh, how welcome breathes the strain!
  Wakening thoughts that long have slept,
Lighting former smiles again
  In faded eyes that long have wept.

MOORE.

She sat by her chamber window,
  The night was calm and fair,
And sweet perfumes from the garden
  Were borne on the quiet air.

Weeping, ceaselessly weeping,
  As the silent hours went by,
Till her dim eyes saw no longer
  One star in the tranquil sky.

There came through night's breathless stillness
  A chime from the old church tower;
She never heard it, nor heeded
  The lapse of the midnight hour.

Till softly, softly, and distant,
  A faint sound stole to her ear;
But she sighed, "It was only the whisper
  Of a breeze that wandered near!"

She sighed, "It was but the night-wind,"
  Yet still she waited to hear,
And again the sweet sound floated
  More sweet to her list'ning ear.

Nearer and nearer coming,
  Yet still like some fairy strain,
Now in the distance dying,
  Now breathing to life again.

Nearer, and ever nearer,
  The sweet sounds come and go,
Till she heard the wheels of a carriage
  Roll over the road below.

Until, in the bright clear starlight,
  She saw it pass her by,
And the horn still softly breathing
  Its strain to the midnight sky.

But the tender spell of the music,
  The strain she had loved to hear
In the distant home of her childhood,
  Had scattered her musings drear ;

For it seemed, in the land of strangers,
  The voice of a cherished friend,
And brighter thoughts of the future
  Began with its notes to blend ;

And a whisper, soft as the falling
  Of roseleaves in summer's prime,
That told her of One great presence
  Unaltered by space or time.

The window was closed, but already
  One upward glance she had given,
And seen that the same sweet message
  Shone down from the stars of heaven.

ENGLAND.

Oh ma patrie,
La plus chérie,
Qui a nourri ma jeune enfance!
MARY QUEEN OF SCOTS.

I cannot close my cherished task,
Or turn to other thoughts away;
Fond memory will not cease to ask
For thee one earnest, heartfelt lay.
Oh, for a tongue of poet-fire
To sing thee, as thou shouldst be sung!
Then, ere its grateful notes expire,
About thine altars should be flung
One wreath of melody divine,
Fit offering for a hallowed shrine.

But thou, whose smile serenely bright
Blent with the sunrise of my days,
Wilt not disdain the tribute slight
That I can render to thy praise.
A child amid thy fair domain
I learned the story of thy past,
While, at each page, the patriot chain
Its golden fetters o'er me cast;
Strong, as the life with which they twine,
These fetters made, and keep me, thine!

It is not that I cannot see
  In other lands the brave and good,
Nor that I hold all right to be
  Engirt by thy surrounding flood;
Let other lands be great and fair,
  And other skies more clear than thine,
Yet, not for all of rich or rare,
  Would I exchange the rays that shine
Bright with the favouring smile of God
  Upon thy throne, thy church, thy sod.

Heart cherished home! no length of years
  Divorces that sweet name from thee;
One changeless love my bosom bears,—
  Star of the Ocean! 'tis for thee.
Till Fate my destined thread has spun,
  Till hopes and fears for me are o'er,
Till Life's last trickling sand has run,
  Although I tread thy fields no more,
While from afar I see thee shine,
  My heart's devotion shall be thine!

PART III.

Leaves from the Wayside.

To Thee I consecrate my lays,
  To whom my powers belong;
These gifts upon Thine altar strown,
O God, accept—accept Thine own.

MONTGOMERY.

Leaves from the Wayside.

"ABIDE WITH US."

Abide with us—the hours of day are waning,
And gloomy skies proclaim th' approach of night;
Leave us not yet, but, with us still abiding,
Cheer us until the morning's welcome light.

Abide with us—before Thy gentle teaching
The crowd of grief that wrapped our spirits fly,
And to our inmost souls thine influence reaching
Lays all our unbelief and terror by.

Abide with us—oh! when our hearts were failing,
How did Thy words revive our dying faith,
The hidden prophecies of old unveiling,
Showing the mysteries of Messiah's death.

Abide with us—so prayed they, though unknowing
Him who had cheered them with His words divine;
So, Lord, with us abide, Thy peace bestowing
Till every heart become thy living shrine.

THE DAY DAWN.

As when the heavy shades of night
  Begin to yield before the dawn,
And first a grey and misty light
  Creeps slowly over grove and lawn,
Until above the purpled hills
  Long level rays their glory pour,
And light the whole wide circle fills,
  And life, where all seemed dead before,

So slowly bright'ning o'er the soul
  Until the shadows flee away,
While night's dark clouds asunder roll
  And fade amid the perfect day,
Dost Thou, O Sun and Light Divine,
  In growing splendour clearly rise,
And bid the heavenly landscape shine
  Refulgent on our wondering eyes.

EVER WITH THEE.

No more in darkness, trials, and temptations,
No more a waif on trouble's billowy sea,
How sweet will be the day of my abiding
Ever with Thee!

Bright after darkness shines the summer morning,
Bright is the sunshine when the tempests flee,
But brighter far the home where dwell Thy chosen
Ever with Thee.

Dear are the hours when those we love are near us,
Dear, but how transient must their brightness be!
That one glad day will know no sadder morrow
Ever with Thee.

Love will be there—methinks all other glories
Nothing to those enraptured souls will be,
Filled with the transport of that one assurance,
Ever with Thee.

But long may be the way that we must travel,
And many a dark'ning storm we yet may see,
Dread sorrows may o'erwhelm us ere we're sheltered
Ever with Thee.

Not so : Thy hand, extended Through the darkness
Leadeth us on the way we cannot see,
And, clasping that, e'en here we walk in safety
Ever with Thee.

"TOUCHED WITH THE FEELING OF OUR INFIRMITIES."

Thou givest the morning's early dew,
The day's awakening light,
The noontide beam, the cool of eve,
The stillness of the night ;
Thou daily dost our strength renew,
And, when our labours close,
Thou watchest by the silent couch
And guardest our repose.

Is there a thought within our brain,
A fancy unexpressed,
That will not clothe itself in words
To mortal ears addressed ?
Yet Thou hast seen it from its rise
And read'st, whate'er it be,
And even the visions of our sleep
Are known, O Lord ! to Thee.

Have we a grief in silence bore
  No human eye can see,
Blooms there a joy within our hearts
  We breathe not e'en to Thee?
Thou seest, thou feel'st, and giv'st us back,
  Alike in joy or woe,
A thrill of finer sympathy
  Than earth can e'er bestow.

Oh! this, beyond the richest store
  Of outward gifts divine,
This proves to many a grateful soul
  That boundless love of Thine;
A love that guards through childhood's years,
  That cheers Life's devious way,
And bears from Death's victorious dart
  The venomed sting away.

THE DEATH OF THE RIGHTEOUS.

"The end of that man is peace."

His end is peace—no more distrest
By cares that harassed him before,
The sunshine of the land of rest
Steals brightly through its open door,
And e'en upon his dying bed
That glorious light is softly shed.

Ah! happy he who early gives
To God the offering of his heart,
For, stayed on him, in peace he lives,
And hails the summons to depart,
And, journeying to so bright a bourne,
For him we cannot, dare not mourn.

The rich man's pomp, the poor man's fare,
Alike are tending to decay;
All earthly pride, all earthly care,
At death's dark hour must pass away;
But happy those, when all is past,
Who win the peace of Heaven at last.

The perfect man, whose soul, refined
By long communion with the sky,
Has left the aims of earth behind
And placed his wealth and hopes on high,
How glorious is his parting hour,
When sin and death have lost their power!

When Jesus, crucified for men,
Was hanging on that dreadful tree,
He blessed the dying thief who then
Pleaded, "O Lord, remember me!"
The Saviour bid his sorrows cease,
And even his last breath was peace.

"I BELIEVE IN THE COMMUNION OF SAINTS."

What is it ? Hast thou ever been 'mong those who roam afar,
Whose unforgotton household fires gleam on them like a star,
A guiding star, that glitters still to show a haven blest,
Where the wanderer yet may moor his bark, the weary yet
may rest ?

Hast thou marked them when they spoke of home, and seen
the flushing brow,
The eyes that soften now with tears, and now with pleasure
glow ?
The voice whose earnest tones grow sweet with music of the
soul,
As mighty tides of love and hope across the bosom roll ?

Oh, I have seen the happy smiles that childhood used to wear,
Come back to brighten for a while the man's pale brow of care,
As thought's bright magic pencil wrought a picture half divine,
Of home, and all the thousand joys round childhood's home
that twine.

And not less dear the Christian's home, that blessed land,
should be
To him who hopes its golden streets, its living streams, to see;
The breathings of its summer air should reach him even now,
And light the smile upon his lip, the gladness on his brow.

Then, when the travellers to that land should hold communion here,
How blest, how glad, those hours would be! how sacred and
how dear!
Nor weariness nor cold restraint to cloud their brightness come,
Forgotten, while the full heart holds no thought but that of
home.

THE HEARER OF PRAYER.

Of all the names beneath the heaven,
Which is the fittest to be given
To Him who rules on High?
What words that mortal lips can frame
Are least unworthy of Thy fame,
Great Lord of earth and sky?

In vain we seek to shadow forth
Thy power, Thy truth, Thy matchless worth,
Thy love, Thy ceaseless care;
To inspiration's page we turn
And there the words in glory burn,
"O Thou that hearest prayer?"

Not all the eloquence sublime
That graced each sage of earlier time
Such words could e'er devise,
Mighty to bind with viewless chain
Man's spirit to his God again
To draw him to the skies.

Poor wand'rers on life's darkling way,
Uncertain still, and apt to stray,
Unsafe, whate'er our care,
It is a blessed thought indeed,
That Thou art near us in our need,
That Thou dost hear our prayer.

The angel hosts that round Thee fly
Exalt Thy praise above the sky
And fill the heavenly air;
But sweeter notes shall swell the hymn
When saints redeemed shall worship Him
Through whom Thou hearest prayer.

THE LAMB IS THE LIGHT THEREOF.

The fairest light that ever shone
In summer skies,
The purest rays that ever flashed
On mortal eyes,
Shall be but as the dead of night
To that eternal, glorious light
That shall be given
To those who, for a little space,
Have bravely run the Christian race
And entered Heav'n.

Sometimes a gleam of that pure light
Is found below
In humble hearts that on their way
With patience go.
It makes those hearts with rapture bound;
And, though the scene be dark around,
It cheers them on,
Augments and brightens day by day,
And still emits a purer ray,
Till life is done.

That spotless sun, which ever lights
Heaven's peaceful clime,
Which no mutation knows, nor shade
Of night or time,
Is but the reflex of His love
Who, slain for us, now reigns above,
Our Saviour-God:
And, while on high His glory's shed,
He guides the pilgrim feet that tread
Where once he trod.

THE SIXTEENTH PSALM.

Preserve me, Lord, for in Thy strength
My trust shall ever be;
My soul with childlike faith and trust,
Shall still repose on Thee.

Thy saints are dear unto my heart,
And those that love Thy way;
But from the dangerous paths of sin
I'll turn my eyes away.

Thou Lord, Thyself, shall be my lot,
And, while Thy love is mine,
I'm owner of a fair domain
A heritage divine.

For this my heart shall still rejoice,
For this my songs shall rise,
Nor death shall chill the certain hope
That points to yonder skies.

Thy power can break his icy chains,
Can set his prisoners free,
And raise the souls that Thou hast made
To dwell in Heaven with Thee.

NIGHT MUSINGS.

Now Night has closed around us,
  And Sleep her wings has spread
O'er many a silent pillow
  O'er many a weary head,
And thousand changeful visions
  Through Fancy's mazes stray,
Where mingle forms of Faëry
  With those of yesterday.

No dreams can weave their network
  Around my brain to-night,
No fancied forms are treading
  That path of silver light;
The moon of Thy ordaining,
  The stars that own Thy word,
Look through my window, telling
  The goodness of the Lord.

Nor they alone are speaking
  Their mighty Maker's praise,
While each eventful moment
  Thy fixed decree obeys;
The breathing of the sleepers,
  The stillness of the hour,
The calm that reigns about us,
  Attest Thy Love and Power.

LIFE'S PILGRIMS.

Pilgrim! that passest by this narrow road,
Dost thou go silent, sorrowing all the day?
Consider 'twas not singing that did stay
Thy feet, that so more swiftly might have trod.
Lift up thy heart in thankful praise to God!
For He, who placed thee in a rugged way,
Hath given thee strength and guidance, and the ray
Of Heaven's pure light to cheer thee, and hath showed
The golden crown that waits thee at the end.
Rejoice! it is thy heritage—rejoice!
Go ever with thanksgiving in thy heart,
So shall thy worship to His throne ascend,
So shall thy heart grow purer, and thy voice
Learn in the angels' songs to bear its part.

THE END.

LIST OF SUBSCRIBERS.

LIST OF SUBSCRIBERS.

Adams, J., Esq.

Ainge, Mrs., England, 2 copies.

Anderson, Mr., United States.

Anderson, Rev. D., M.A.

Armour, Mr.

Armstrong, Rev. D., 2 copies.

Baird, Mrs., 2 copies.

Baird, Rev. R. G., 3 copies.

Barr, Miss, United States, 2 copies.

Becher, H. C. R., Esq., 2 copies.

Birrell, Mr. D., United States, 2 copies.

Black, Mr.

Boone, Mr., United States, 2 copies.

Bowen, Rev. S., England, 5 copies.

Breakey, Mr. W.

Bridges, C. J., Esq., 2 copies.

Bucke, Dr.

Bucke, Mr. Julius P.

Burke, J. W., Esq., P.L.S., 2 copies.

Cameron, Hon. M., 2 copies.

Campbell, J. D., Esq., 2 copies.

Carman, Mr.

Caw, Rev. D.

Clark.,Mr. W B.

Clarke, Duncan, Esq., 2 copies.

Corser, Mrs., England, 2 copies.

Cox, Mr. W., United States, 2 copies.

Crawford, Mr., 2 copies.

Crawford, Mrs. W., United States.

Dartmouth, the Earl of, 4 copies.

Davenport, Mrs. J., England.

Davie, Miss.

Davie, Mrs.

Davis, Miss.

Davis, Miss L. C., 6 copies.

Dougall, Mrs. F., United States.

Durham, Miss.

Elliot, Mr., 10 copies.

Ellis, Mrs.

Esden, Mrs., 2 copies.

Evans, Mr. P. C., England.

Evans, Rev. W. B.

Farrell, Mrs. S. W.

Fleming, Mr.

Flintoft, Mrs.

Fowler, Mrs., England.

Frazer, Rev. G., B.D., England.

Gemmill, Mr. D.
Glass, Mrs.
Haden, Rev. A. B., M.A., England, 4 copies.
Hartland, Miss, England.
Hartley, Mrs. J., England, 7 copies.
Haws, Mrs. G. W.
Hay, Mrs., England, 10 copies.
Heard, Mr., United States.
Higham, Miss, England, 2 copies.
Higham, Miss E., 2 copies.
Higham, Miss S. A., 2 copies.
Higham, Mr. F., 2 copies.
Higham, Mr. G., 2 copies.
Inglis, Dr. R., United States.
Inglis, Rev. D., 4 copies.
Inglis, Rev. J.
Irving, Æmilius, Esq., 2 copies.
Jamieson, Mr. A.
Jamieson, Mr. R. A.
Jamieson, Rev. A.
Jenkins, Rev. J. H., B.A., 2 copies.
Kemp, Rev. A. F., 6 copies.
Kerr, Mr. D. R., 2 copies.
Kerr, Mrs. D. R.
Kerr, Mrs. G., England.
Lawson, Miss.
Lewis, Mr., England, 4 copies.
Lister, Mrs., England.

Lloyd, Miss, 4 copies.
Lloyd, Mrs., 4 copies.
Macalister, Mr. N.
Mackenzie, J. A., Esq.
Marples, Mr., England, 8 copies.
Martin, Mr., 6 copies.
McDonald, Mr., 9 copies.
McInnes, D., Esq., 2 copies.
McLean, Mr. A.
McLean, Mr. G.
McMullen, Mr.
McMurray, H., Esq., 2 copies.
McNab, A., Esq.
McNaughton, Miss.
McVicar, Mr.
Mitchell, Mr. J., 2 copies.
Monckton, Major J., England, 2 copies.
Monckton, Miss, 2 copies.
Monckton, Miss E. L.
Monckton, Miss Fanny.
Monckton, Miss Rosa, 4 copies.
Monckton, Mrs., 2 copies.
Monckton, W., Esq., 8 copies.
Murray, Rev. J.
Padfield, Mr.
Padfield, Mr. A.
Parke, Mr., England, 2 copies.
Patton, Miss.

Patton, Mr. H. N.
Patton, Mrs. H. N.
Peckham, Judge, U. S.
Pizey, Rev. E., B.A., England.
Plant, Miss, England.
Pope, Miss.
Pope, Miss E.
Pope, Mrs., United States.
Poussett, Mr. H.
Poussett, P. T., Esq.
Rainsberry, Mr.
Reekie, Mrs.
Reynolds, Mr. G., England.
Reynolds, T., Esq., 12 copies.
Robson, Mr. D.
Roe, Rev. H., B.A., 2 copies.
Sawyer, Rev. W. G., England, 8 copies.
Shoebotham, Dr., 2 copies.
Siddens, Miss, England.
Sloan, Mr., United States.
Smith, J., Esq., England, 20 copies.
Speary, Mrs., England.
Stephens, W. C., Esq., 2 copies.
Stewart, Mrs., United States.
Stokes, Mrs., 2 copies.
Sullivan, Mrs.
Symington, Mr.
Talfourd, F., Esq.

Thorneycroft, Mrs. T., England, 2 copies.
Thornton, Mr.
Thorp, Rev. W., England.
Toogood, Miss, England.
Townley, Rev. A., D.D.
Trubshaw, Mr. J., United States, 2 copies.
Turnbull, Mrs.
Vidal, Mrs.
Walsh, Rev. W., England.
Ward, Mr. G.
Warren, Mr., United States.
Watson, Mrs. E. P.
Wheelock, Mr., United States, 2 copies.
Whichcote, General, England, 8 copies.
Williams, Mr.
Woodall, Mr. W., England, 40 copies.
Wright, Miss.
Young, Mr. A.
Young, Mr. H.

www.ingramcontent.com/pod-product-compliance
Lightning Source LLC
Chambersburg PA
CBHW030900050726
47500CB00009B/427
9783744642361